# Murder in Seabrook Shores

*A Samantha Degan Mystery*

by

Jane O'Brien

For information, email **Cozy Cat Press**, cozycatpress@aol.com  or visit our website at: www.cozycatpress.com

**COZY CAT PRESS**

ISBN:  978-1-946063-19-9

Printed in the United States of America

Cover design by Paula Ellenberger
www.paulaellenberger.com

1 2 3 4 5 6 7 8 9 10

A big thank you those who encourage me in my writing. I hope everyone enjoys reading about Samantha's adventures as much as I enjoy writing them.

PROLOGUE

After circling for twenty minutes in the air at LAX, the airplane landed smoothly.

Samantha Degan and her assistant, Megan Fairchild, made their way through the terminal to the baggage claim area.

"Samantha, look," Megan whispered. "That man is holding a sign with your name on it."

Samantha smiled. "That's our ride. I'd better let him know we've arrived."

Samantha preferred her new name—Samantha Fletcher, since her marriage six months ago to Detective Joseph Fletcher. However, as a mystery writer with novels published with her maiden name, her agent, Marco Branch had cautioned her not to make changes.

*****

While completing her education at the University of Lancashire, Samantha had worked as an assistant to Professor Fenwick Stonehill. The professor was a semi-invalid, octogenarian who was writing his memoirs. After his untimely death, Samantha finished the chronicle of the professor's complicated and fascinating life. His biography was the reason she and Megan were in Los Angeles. A movie studio had purchased Professor Stonehill's story.

Samantha had been given a fully paid trip for two to California as a consultant on the movie set. Her husband Fletch was a detective on the Lancashire Police force and unable leave his job for any length of time, so Samantha had invited her assistant, Megan, to go to California with her.

Samantha was thrilled when Marco called to say Hollywood wanted to tell the professor's story. However, her enthusiasm began to fade when she questioned why a movie company was interested in a professor who was well-known only in the Lancashire area.

*****

Megan was happy to be in California in February. It had been an especially cold and snowy January, and it didn't seem February would be any better. Megan had never been to California and was looking forward to seeing movie stars and palm trees.

As the limousine traveled to the hotel on the busy freeway, Megan gazed out her window, disappointed that she was not able to recognize a single face as the cars sped past her. She was beginning to miss Lancashire and Mike Thompson. Megan had met Mike when she'd begun working for Samantha in her apartment office. Mike lived across the hall in the same building. Shortly after her relationship with the abusive Jimmy Lee Baker had ended, she and Mike became an item. He asked her to give some serious thought to marriage while she was away. If she lived through this ride, she planned to accept his proposal when she returned to Lancashire.

"Samantha, I've never seen so many cars in one place. I thought I'd like to rent a car and see the sights, but I'd be too nervous on these roads. I'm afraid to see what speed we're going."

"We'd better get used to it," Samantha said anxiously, "it's only one o'clock in the afternoon. Imagine how bad it will be at rush hour."

To their relief, they made it to the hotel in one piece.

# CHAPTER 1

Samantha and Megan tried their best to not look like tourists as they rode the elevator to their suite on the twenty-fourth floor in the exclusive Hotel Lexington.

After living in the luxurious Stonehill Manor for the better part of a year, Samantha wasn't completely in awe of the glitz and glamor of the hotel lobby. The sun shining through the massive windows accentuated the richness of the furnishings and reflected off the glass chandelier on the ceiling in the center of the room.

The bellman opened the door to their suite, revealing a luxurious living room with a winding staircase to the second-floor bedrooms.

Chilled champagne was waiting for them along with a large bouquet of flowers and a basket of assorted fresh fruit.

After depositing their luggage in the proper bedrooms, the bellman declined Samantha's offer of a tip.

"Pinch me," Megan squealed. "This is like being in a dream. If only the guys could see us now."

"I never expected anything like this when Marco told me our room would be paid for. I thought first class seats on the airplane were a mistake, but now I'm beginning to wonder."

"Let's just enjoy it, Samantha, before they figure out we're nobodies and ship us off to a two-star motel on the outskirts of town."

"I have a little extra time to call Fletch to let him know we arrived safely. Marco said the screenwriter, Grant Wagner, won't arrive until two o'clock."

*****

"Detective Fletcher," Fletch answered the phone in his usual curt way.

"Hello, Detective, this is Mrs. Fletcher, calling from a luxurious hotel in sunny California."

"Hey, sweetheart, it's good to hear your voice; how's California?"

"It's a beautiful seventy-four degrees, the sun is shining, but I miss you."

"It's snowing here and I miss you too."

"Fletch, you wouldn't believe the place where we're staying; it's a luxurious two-story suite. I wish you could be here to enjoy it with me."

"I wish I was there to enjoy you."

Samantha was an old married woman of six months, but her heart still fluttered at the sound of his provocative words. She hoped it would always be that way.

*****

At precisely two o'clock, Grant Wagner called from the lobby.

Samantha told him to come to the suite where it was quiet and they'd have more privacy.

Megan answered the knock at the door. "Mr. Wagner, I'm Megan Fairbanks, Ms. Degan's assistant; please come in.

It surprised Samantha to see a young man, not more than twenty-five entered the room.

"Ms. Degan, I'm Grant Wagner." He held out his hand.

"Please call me Samantha; may I call you Grant? I think we'll be working together for the next several weeks, and I think *Mr.* and *Ms.* sound too formal, don't you?"

"I'd like that, Samantha. I read your book and found it to be a genuine story of Professor Stonehill; he was an interesting man and led an interesting life. I think I should warn you, though, his life on screen will not resemble his life as you wrote it."

"I understand changes are necessary to adapt the story to a screenplay, but I'm sure you won't change the professor's character."

"Samantha, why did you choose to sell the rights to your book?"

"My agent, Marco Branch, told me there was an offer to buy the book to make a film. I thought it would be a nice tribute to Professor Stonehill."

"Did he tell you who bought the rights?"

"No, I assumed it was the studio."

"It's an old guy they call Mr. C. His young wife decided she wanted stardom and he bought your story for her. I have orders to make her a more prominent figure in the professor's life. I doubt you intended to be portrayed as Professor Stonehill's mistress."

Samantha couldn't believe she was hearing Grant's words correctly. That feeling of apprehension about the movie returned in that moment.

"That's disgusting; you can't write that about the professor. He was a decent and honest man; he would never have used a woman like that."

"I followed my instructions. Mr. C's wife's name is Rochelle Rousseau I haven't met her, but I hear she's a beauty, and close to sixty years younger than Mr. C."

"I want to talk to this Mr. C; he can't do this to Professor Stonehill."

"He's not doing it to Professor Stonehill; he's doing it to Professor Hill. Every name in your book has been edited to avoid controversy. I don't like the outcome any better than you do, but I need the money. If I didn't write the revisions, they'd just get someone else to do it. This town isn't easy on writers and I had to take what I could get."

"At the cost of your integrity, Grant?"

"I'm afraid I lost that when I couldn't come up with my rent payment this month. I was forced to borrow from my folks or risk being on the street. After this, they'll only send me money for a plane ticket home. This is my last chance to make a name for myself here. You and Megan should pack up your things and take the first plane out of here before you get sucked into this life," he said, glancing around the pretentious room.

"Samantha," said Megan, "why don't I call the airline. We can get the first flight out tomorrow. Let's go home; I've seen my fill of palm trees and I've lost interest in looking for movie stars."

"I can't leave yet, Megan. Not without talking to this Mr. C. Maybe I can make him understand that the professor deserves to be treated like the respectable man he was."

"If I can't talk you out of staying here, let me at least drive you to the Seabrook Estate. It's on Seabrook Shores, an exclusive area facing the Pacific. From pictures I've seen of Stonehill Manor, the resemblance is amazing."

Megan was leery of going anywhere with Grant. She didn't trust him after he admitted he ruined Samantha's beautiful story of an honorable man. Even so, the two women followed the young man out of the hotel and to his car.

"Fletch and Mike would want us to be careful of this man," she whispered in Samantha's ear. "If you insist on going with him, I'll go too, but I hope he doesn't murder us on the way."

"Megan, don't be so suspicious. I think you've been around me too long. Grant seems like a nice young man who isn't willing to give up his dream; we'll be fine."

Grant's car was over twenty years old with a faded paint job. *It didn't look like it would survive on that horrible freeway,* Megan thought to herself as she sat in the back seat and fastened her seat belt. She was surprised the car started at all.

As though he could read her mind, Grant told the women that his dad was a mechanic and he'd learned how to take care of a car at an early age.

"Where are you from, Grant?" Samantha asked.

"It's a small town in Iowa; I left there ten months ago," he said with melancholy in his voice.

"It sounds like you miss it," said Megan.

"I do, but I can't go back as a failure; if this job doesn't work out, I won't have a choice."

"Did you leave a girl back home?" asked Samantha.

"How did you guess? It's true, I did leave a girl. She's the daughter of the wealthiest man in town. Stuart Reed is the only bank's president, and Jennifer is his only child. I know she loves me, but I can't offer her more than a mechanic's salary and she's always been treated like a princess."

"Grant, I haven't read your work, but you must have talent if this Mr. C. hired you as a screenwriter for my book."

"I do have talent, but I've had more rejection notices than I can count. I want to write, but I also like to eat and I don't seem to be able to do both."

*****

Samantha understood the frustration she heard in Grant's voice. Professor Stonehill's memoirs opened the door for her and her mysteries. He was such a celebrated figure in Lancashire that the books were big sellers there.

Megan was beginning to have second thoughts about Grant's character and wondered if Jennifer was worthy of him. To her relief, they exited the congested freeway and traveled a winding road until the ocean came into view.

Grant turned into a long driveway with colorful flowers, lush green bushes, and well-pruned fruit trees along the way. They could see tall palm trees in the distance and heard the ocean.

As they drove closer to the house at the end of the driveway, Samantha gasped. Grant was right; it looked exactly like Stonehill Manor.

"How did you ever find this place? Except for the landscaping, I would swear we were looking at the professor's mansion," cried Samantha.

CHAPTER 2

Grant pulled up to the front entrance of the house and opened the door to step out.

"Come on; don't you want to see the inside?"

"Grant, it's someone's home; we can't just walk in."

"Sure we can; the owner has leased it to the studio while he's in Europe. The set designer's waiting for us; she wants to make this place into a replica of Stonehill Manor. Do you think you can remember the details of the mansion in Lancashire, Samantha?"

"I'm sure I can," Samantha said. Her heart pounded because the place brought back many memories of her time with the professor and after his death.

A tall, stylish woman in her early forties swung open the door. She was wearing a long sweeping flowered skirt with a sheer blouse and a short-sleeved bolero shrug jacket.

"Welcome to Seabrook Estate; I'm Myra Sims; you may call me Myra. I've been so anxious to meet you, Samantha. I've read your book and can picture Stonehill Manor in my mind. As you can see," Myra prattled on, "the former owners had expensive taste, but the furnishings are nothing like the dear professor's dwelling."

"I have several sketches lined up for you to see. I hope you'll find the perfect matches for every piece of furniture in the mansion when you lived there."

Samantha was speechless. Except for the furniture and artwork, the first floor sketch was identical to Stonehill Manor. The double stairway with an elevator in the center brought back memories of the professor coming down to the main floor from his office. She could picture the delicately ornate elevator door opening and George pushing the professor's wheelchair through it.

"Whoever built this house must have had a copy of Stonehill Manor's blueprints. It can't be a coincidence," Samantha said.

"The story goes that Hawthorne Stonehill, Fenwick's father, came to California on business some sixty or more years ago. He met a dancer named Jasmine Flowers. Poor Hawthorne was so smitten with Jasmine that he planned to leave his wife, Maybelle, and their teenaged son, and move to California to marry Jasmine. As it turned out, after thinking her childbearing years were behind her, Maybelle became pregnant with Fenwick's sister, Eliza. Hawthorne did the honorable thing and stayed with Maybelle.

"Jasmine was furious when Hawthorne told her they couldn't be married after all. She vowed to tell Maybelle the truth unless he paid, and paid dearly for her silence. Hawthorne was horrified to learn what a selfish, vengeful woman Jasmine had become.

"She arrived at the doorstep of Stonehill Manor. Fortunately, Maybelle was not home at the time. Jasmine insisted on seeing every room in the house and announced she expected Hawthorne to build her a mansion just like it overlooking the Pacific Ocean.

"Hawthorne Stonehill was a wealthy man but having a replica of Stonehill Manor built was an expensive undertaking. To save his marriage, he felt he had no choice and agreed to do as Jasmine ordered. Hawthorne's love for his beautiful flower faded. Trying to rid himself of her memory, he signed the title to the mansion over to Jasmine and washed his hands of the entire matter.

"After the home was built, Jasmine found she missed the action of the city and resented being stuck in the dreary mansion with nothing but servants to keep her company. She sold the house and moved to a luxurious apartment in Los Angeles. She continued her dance career and eventually met and married Addison Lambert. Eventually, Jasmine moved with him to London where she gave birth to twin sons. Addison wasn't a pushover like his predecessor and Jasmine was forced to behave herself. Her mother-in-law saw potential in her son's new wife and made it her life's mission to transform her into a lady befitting the Lambert name.

"Blake Lambert is the grandson of the late Jasmine Lambert. He loved hearing stories about the parties and galas held at the Seabrook mansion when his grandmother was young and beautiful. As he grew older, he suspected the stories were figments of his grandmother's imagination but still listened intently to her tales.

"Blake's business dealings brought him to Los Angeles where he searched for and found the mansion. It had been abandoned and in slight disrepair. In memory of his late grandmother, Blake bought the house and began repairs. He found he didn't have the time or the inclination to restore it to match the theme of Jasmine's fantasies."

*****

"Myra, that's a fascinating story," said Samantha. "I'm sure the professor never knew about his father's relationship with another woman. I'm glad he didn't know; it would have crushed him. Does the house stand empty when Mr. Lambert is out of the country?"

"I'm afraid so; a cleaning crew comes in once a week, but most often, it's empty. I understand Mr. Lambert has a small place in the city. Now, I have the sketches laid out on the dining room table if you will follow me, please."

Only four areas were going to be staged for use in the film. They included the library, the professor's suite, the large foyer and the suite used by Samantha.

Samantha looked over the sketches. "I don't think it's necessary to recreate the suite of rooms I was in; there's so little in the book about that room except the kidnapping of Mari."

"That suite is pivotal to the story, Samantha. Our heroine enjoyed many pleasurable hours in her boudoir," laughed Myra.

Samantha glared at Grant in disgust. "What kind of person are you painting me to be, Grant? There's nothing in my book suggesting promiscuity took place in that room."

"That's not true, Samantha," said Myra. "It was obvious your bed had a special meaning to you. So much so that you took it with you when you left the mansion."

"That's ridiculous; I loved that bed because it was luxurious. I didn't take it with me; it was given to me. It is now in the guest room of the house I share with my husband. Do you honestly think I would keep it in my home if I'd shared it with other men as you are suggesting?"

"Look, Samantha," Myra said, shaking her head, "we're making a current movie here, not some old Doris and Rock flick from the fifties. The audience wants to watch sex and that's what they will see. We're in this to make money and we'll do what it takes to make plenty of it."

"I can't let you ruin the reputation of an extraordinary man. I want to talk to Mr. C, whoever he is. How can I get in touch with him?"

"Samantha, I don't know the man. I only know he's paying for my services. If you don't want to tell me what your bedroom looked like, so be it. I'll do what I must do to make it look authentic. Now, help me with the other sketches."

"No, Myra, I won't be a party to this disgusting travesty. Grant, please take us back to the hotel. Megan and I will be checking out and returning to Lancashire."

"Samantha, calm down," said Myra, "it's not what you think. I've read Grant's script and it's a very sensitive and meaningful play. Yes, he did spice it up some, but that is what the audience wants. Please, give it some time; don't give up yet."

Myra's words did calm Samantha somewhat. She was furious with herself for selling out. In her quest to honor the beloved professor, she had become a part in mocking his life.

"Samantha," said Grant, "I know this is difficult for you. You're not the only author who's been disturbed by adjustments in a piece written from your heart. I wish you would reconsider; I believe you'll have a positive influence with Barry Kline, the director who Mr. C has assigned to the project."

"Grant, I must speak with Mr. C. I have to make him understand the kind of man Professor Stonehill was. Someone must know how to get in touch with him."

"You'll be meeting Melvin Kessler this evening; he's the producer. He's a difficult man, but he's the only person who has the power to make changes. Mr. C is an enigma from what I've heard and has nothing to do with the production."

Samantha apologized for overreacting and studied Myra's sketches, selecting those that most resembled the original Stonehill Manor. She offered some suggestions as she remembered details of the décor.

## CHAPTER 3

On the way back to the city, Grant suggested Samantha and Megan rest in their suite for an hour before the cocktail party being held in one of the meeting rooms in the hotel.

"Remember, it's a three-hour time difference there in California. I should have waited until tomorrow before I drove you to Seabrook."

Samantha was still uneasy about the portrayal of the professor. She would call Fletch when they returned to the hotel to ask his opinion about the situation. She wondered if anything could be done to stop the production. After all, she had sold the rights to her book. *How could I have been so naïve?* she wondered. *I thought they would strictly adhere to my words. I'm sorry, Professor*, she thought to herself.

*****

Megan had never met Professor Stonehill, but she knew how highly regarded he'd been throughout his life.

What began as an exciting adventure to share with her friend and employer, had taken a disturbing turn. Megan hoped Samantha would be able to persuade the decision makers to tone down the sexual inferences in the movie. She had no doubt Samantha was not guilty of improprieties while living at Stonehill Manor.

*****

"Fletch, I'm afraid I've made a terrible mistake," Samantha said when she called Fletch after returning to the hotel. "I haven't read the script, but it's no longer the true story of the dedicated and honorable man I knew. My first thought was to return to Lancashire, but I'm hoping to convince the decision makers to change their minds about this version."

"You said the screenwriter was the one who drove you and Megan to the Seabrook mansion. What does he say about the revisions?"

"Grant is young and trying to make a success of his writing. He doesn't think he has a choice and is giving them what they want. I can't blame him; it seems sex is what sells out here. I know you had reservations about selling my rights to the book and now I wish I'd gone with your instincts."

"Do you want me to come out there? I hate that you're alone to face these people. I'll take a leave from the force if I have to."

"No, don't do that. I know you and Mike are planning to join us later in the month. Maybe everything will work out by that time and we can have the vacation we planned. Tonight is a cocktail party where we'll be meeting the director and producer. Grant tells us the actors will be there too. I'm anxious to meet the actress who will be portraying me. Grant heard she's a fox," Samantha giggled.

"Of course, she's a fox. She's playing the part of you. But no matter who she is, she won't measure up to my best girl."

"You're good for my ego; I miss you, but it's time to get dressed for this shindig tonight. I'd call you later, but you'll be asleep, I'm sure."

"I won't sleep that well without you by my side; call me no matter what time it is. I want to hear about your evening."

*****

Samantha looked stunning in a simple but elegant deep blue cocktail length dress. She wore the diamond pendant Fletch had given her for their six-month anniversary. Megan was dressed in soft green A-line that brought out the color of her eyes and accentuated her blonde hair. They stood before the floor length mirror hoping they would fit in with the sophisticated crowd at the party.

*****

The room was almost empty when they entered at ten minutes after seven. Grant saw them walk in and greeted them with a smile.

"Where is everyone?" Samantha asked. "I thought there would be more people here."

"They'll be arriving soon; movie people like to make grand entrances. I came early to fortify myself to deal with the egomaniacs." He held up a half-full glass of bourbon. "May I get you ladies a drink?"

"I'll have a glass of white wine. I'd better drink lightly tonight; I don't need a loose tongue when I talk to the bigwigs," said Samantha.

Megan asked for the same. Grant returned with the wine when Melvin Kessler entered the room. He had a scowl on his face and was glancing around the room as though he was looking for someone.

Grant took another generous swig of his drink before he guided Samantha and Megan to the newcomer.

"Mr. Kessler, may I introduce Samantha Degan and her assistant, Megan Fairchild. Samantha is the author of *Stonehill Manor*."

"I know who she is, Wagner. Get me whatever you're having while I talk with the lovely Ms. Degan."

Grant dutifully walked to the bar as ordered. I hate that guy," he mumbled under his breath.

"It's nice to meet you, Mr. Kessler. I'm glad I have a chance to speak with you about the changes in Professor Stonehill's story. If you've read my book, you know Fenwick Stonehill was a gentleman. I cannot allow the filming of the movie to begin unless the professor's character is true to the man he was throughout his life."

"How many of those have you had, little lady?" Melvin Kessler sneered, while pointing to Samantha's glass of wine. "Need I remind you, you don't own the story of your sainted professor. It was a good mystery, but too sappy for the movie screen. I'm in the business of making money and so's my boss, Mr. C. You stand to collect a small fortune too, but only if we throw sex and violence into the mix."

Grant returned with the man's drink. "Wagner," Mr. Kessler said, "tell your friend to get it together or she'll be on the next bus back to the east coast or wherever she's from."

"I'm sorry, Samantha," whispered Grant, "I should have warned you about Kessler."

"You did mention he was difficult and I should have expected his reaction. I'm not giving up; I find it hard to believe moviegoers are only interested in sex in movies. I hope Mr. C is here tonight; maybe he will be more reasonable."

Megan knew from the look on Grant's face that Samantha was fighting a losing battle. She would talk to her when they were in their suite after the party ended. Because the character in the movie is named Hill, not Stonehill, she hoped the film wouldn't reflect badly on the professor.

*****

More people began to arrive while waiters weaved through the crowd with trays of champagne and tempting appetizers. The bar was knee-deep in those looking for something stronger than sparkling wine.

An attractive man in his late thirties approached Samantha.

"Samantha Degan, I recognize you from your photograph. I'm Barry Kline. I'll be directing Grant's version of your book." He nodded in Grant's direction.

"I'm happy to meet you, Mr. Kline; this is my assistant, Megan Fairchild."

"Please call me Barry; I hope you're both enjoying your stay in Los Angeles."

"Barry," said Samantha, "I will be honest, I'm not enjoying any part of this visit because the true story of Fenwick Stonehill is not being told. I understand your studio wants to make money, but I question why it's necessary to destroy a man's reputation to do so."

"Believe it or not, Samantha, I agree with you," Barry replied. "Grant did his best to please Melvin and keep some of the integrity of your story. Actually, it might have been even worse in the hands of some of the screenwriters I know. After I read your book, I was anxious to direct the movie, but now I regret signing a contract."

*****

A hush came over the room and heads turned toward the door. The most beautiful woman Samantha had ever seen entered on the arm of a gentleman who was several years her senior.

"Do you suppose that's Rochelle Rousseau?" Megan whispered.

"I don't know; who is that Barry? She's beautiful."

"Megan's correct; that's Rochelle with Mr. C. He insists she plays you, Samantha. She's never acted a day in her life. I'm afraid the movie will be a flop before Grant's script is finalized. Come, I'll introduce you."

"I can't believe that gorgeous woman will be playing me. I don't look anything like her." Samantha saw the look on Grant's face as he stared at the glamorous Ms. Rousseau and knew he was a goner.

Barry made the introductions.

"So this is the little author of the sweet professor's story. Samantha, isn't it?"

"Yes, Ms. Rousseau. I'm Samantha Degan Fletcher." Samantha had been called many things in her lifetime but, because she was tall, no one had ever called her *little*.

"Where's your detective? Don't tell me you left him alone in your little hometown?"

*What's with the word* little*? These people use it so often,* Samantha thought, but said: "Fletch will be joining us in a few weeks if we're still in California."

"I'll be anxious to see him," she said and walked toward Grant, putting her arm in his. You must be my screenwriter—Bryant, isn't it, cutie?

"It's Grant, Ms. Rousseau." His face turned bright red as she led him to the bar.

"That woman is giving off evil vibes," said Megan. "I don't think she likes you very much, Samantha."

"I can't imagine what I did to offend her."

"She's probably jealous."

"What would she have to be jealous about?" asked Samantha. "She's beautiful."

"You have natural beauty; hers is bought and paid for by a feeble old man. Her cleavage comes to her navel, maybe she's getting a kickback from her plastic surgeon for advertising his work."

\*\*\*\*\*

The party continued and Rochelle continued to play the room, occasionally scowling in Samantha's direction.

Samantha did her best to ignore the woman and watched for an opportunity to speak with Mr. C. His giant bodyguard remained at his side, watching and waiting as though someone was intent on harming the old gentleman. Walking toward him with the body guard's eyes on her, Samantha introduced herself as the author of Professor Stonehill's memoirs.

"Let her pass, Ivor," Mr. C instructed. "This pretty young lady means me no harm."

"Thank you, Mr. C. I hoped to speak to you about the screenplay of my book. I have been told in order to make money, my original work has been transformed into a movie filled with sex. I can assure you, Professor Fenwick Stonehill was never involved in a scandal of any kind. He was a gentleman, much like yourself, and deserves to be treated with respect and dignity."

Mr. C laughed. "My dear, please don't let this body fool you. In my day I was what we called a *randy*. I'm certain your professor was a fine upstanding gentleman. My lovely wife is too beautiful and sexy to waste her talents on a mundane, boring picture. Now, if you will excuse me."

Samantha knew when she was being dismissed and knew it was useless to talk to this old man. She felt sickened that two of the people who had total control over her story were steadfast in their quest to make the professor out to be a lecher and her no better than a common tramp.

She saw that Rochelle had unhinged herself from Grant. He stood by the window with his eyes glued on the actress.

"Grant, tell me more about the script. I know you changed the professor's name; did you change mine?"

"I did. I called you Savannah, but Rochelle wanted to keep your name, Samantha. Isn't she the most beautiful woman you've ever seen?"

"Grant, listen to me; what other changes are there? Is Detective Fletcher mentioned?"

"Yes, but only as the arresting officer. Rochelle thought it would be more realistic if he was married."

"I thought you'd never met Rochelle until tonight."

"I hadn't. Her assistant told me what changes to make and I did what I was told."

"Thanks, Grant. Remember the girl you left in Iowa? Be careful not to mess that up."

Grant looked at her quizzically and then turned to watch Rochelle with a lovesick look on his face.

"Megan, something's not right here. Am I being paranoid or is Rochelle out to make me look bad?"

"I don't think you're paranoid, Sam. The daggers are coming out of that woman's eyes when she looks your way. I'm sure you'll investigate what's going on with her and why she's intent on trashing you and Professor Stonehill."

## CHAPTER 4

Reggie Crenshaw was no fool. He was aware that Rachel's sudden interest in becoming an actress stemmed from her lingering lust for her cop ex-boyfriend, Joseph Fletcher. He'd gone along with her when she'd insisted on being called Rochelle Rousseau instead of Rachel Ross Crenshaw. He'd also agreed to the idiotic name of *Mr. C.* Reggie wasn't a stupid man, but he *was* a man who couldn't say no to Rachel.

Reggie had had many love interests in his seventy-nine years on earth, but none had had the effect on him that Rachel Ross did. He knew from the beginning that she had feelings for someone else. It didn't matter to Reggie; he was in love and determined to make Rachel his.

Five years ago, he'd proposed marriage although he suspected she anticipated his demise soon and would take up with the cop again when that happened. Reggie was willing to overlook her frequent dalliances; after all, he wasn't the young, virile man he once was. Detective Fletcher was a different matter. Rachel had feelings for him that went beyond her usual flirtations.

Reggie was surprised when Rachel's maid reported finding the *Memoirs of Professor Fenwick Stonehill* on her nightstand. To his knowledge, Rachel had never cracked a book in her life. Her reading material consisted of gossip and celebrity magazines. Reggie quickly ordered his own copy of the biography and immediately recognized the character known as *Fletch*.

Shortly after that, Rachel told him she wanted to be a movie star and insisted he buy the rights to the professor's memoirs. Although Reggie had never been a part of the movie business, he knew many studio heads and found one that was willing to take a chance because Reggie was footing the bill.

He knew the story would have to be rewritten to make Rachel the focus of the movie. He didn't expect the studio he'd convinced to produce the movie would be willing to assign their top screenwriters to the project. However, they did find one fellow who was hungry enough to do what he was told.

The poor jerk was Grant Wagner. Rachel forced him to rewrite his screenplay several times before she gave her approval. Reggie almost felt sorry for the poor sap; he'd sold his soul for nothing. The movie would never be made because Rachel had no talent, but Reggie would let her discover *that* truth for herself.

Even so, Reggie had hired the best in the business to make her dream come true. He couldn't help it if she fell flat on her beautiful face in the process.

After meeting Samantha Degan, Reggie doubted that Detective Fletcher had any lingering feelings for Rachel. Samantha was truly a beautiful woman. She had a style and grace that only comes from someone who has confidence in themselves and a genuine caring for other people. Detective Fletcher was a lucky man. Reggie truly wanted to assure Mrs. Fletcher that she needn't worry about the professor's name being tainted, that no one would ever read about her in an unflattering light. However, he remained silent because he couldn't risk Rachel finding out that her precious movie career would probably be over before it started.

*****

Melvin Kessler knew his days of prosperity were numbered. He was heavily in debt, thanks to alimony and child support because of three divorces. He had no interest in his four children and resented having to foot the bill for their care. He'd been a fool to think he was in love— not once, but three times. His latest love interest was Rochelle Rousseau. She was not only beautiful, but she knew how to make a man feel like a man. If only old Crenshaw would kick, then Rochelle would collect all his money. Melvin and Rochelle could be married and he wouldn't have to worry about finances again.

He wondered why she picked the subject of some old professor in a small town to make her first appearance on the silver screen. It was a good mystery and an interesting story, but the old man was too squeaky clean. That young guy Grant Wagner did a good job of spicing up the screenplay, however, and Melvin was looking forward to watching Rochelle in those bedroom scenes. He wasn't worried about Brad Taylor, the actor who would play the professor. Melvin watched Brad from across the room, he'd been staring at Samantha Degan all evening. Good. Maybe a little distraction with the author would keep Brad from continuing any of the on-screen love scenes with Rochelle after the cameras were turned off.

\*\*\*\*\*

Brad Taylor couldn't take his eyes off the beautiful woman across the room. He was attracted to her hair coloring and the way it swayed when she walked. He was sorry she wasn't playing herself in the movie; he wanted her all to himself. He'd noticed the ring she wore on her left hand, but it didn't matter to him. He would make her forget about every other man she'd ever known.

\*\*\*\*\*

Barry Kline hated these parties. He'd started his career as an actor, but had quickly found he had a knack for directing. He left acting behind and, through luck and determination, found he could make a decent living and provide comfortably for his wife, Andie, and their two children.

The Kline family lived in an upscale neighborhood in the suburbs of Los Angeles where Andie stayed home with the children—five-year-old Benjy and two-year-old Chloe. Life was almost perfect until the day Benjy was diagnosed with leukemia. The cancer had taken a toll on the entire family. The little boy was recovering from the disease and the bills were piling up. Barry carried medical insurance on the family, but his policy was not sufficient to cover the cost of a catastrophic illness.

They were close to losing their home to foreclosure which was the main reason Barry had signed a contract to direct the Stonehill movie.

He knew the movie could be a classic someday if only it kept with the original story. He also knew it might not be profitable if it wasn't embellished with sex.

Andie assured her husband that they'd still be a family even if they had to give up their home. Wherever they lived, they would be grateful that Benjy had survived and would soon be the happy little guy he'd been before the illness. Still, Barry blamed himself for their financial situation. If only he hadn't tried to save a few bucks, their insurance coverage would have been enough and they wouldn't be in this mess.

He determined that he would do his best to make the movie as good as it could be and hoped his reputation as a director wouldn't be irreparably damaged.

*****

Rachel Ross, now known as Rochelle, seethed when she looked in Samantha's direction. She remembered the last time she saw Fletch. She knew she'd broken his heart, but what was she to do? Reggie Crenshaw was in love with her and could give her every comfort imaginable. She didn't love him, but he didn't revile her either. It was bad luck when she fell in love with a cop. How could Fletch expect her to live in a little house in Chicago?

Five years ago, she'd explained to Fletch that Reggie couldn't live forever and once he was gone, they'd be together. Then he could quit his stupid job and they could live in luxury. She was furious that Fletch didn't wait for her to be free. Instead, he married that little nobody— Samantha Degan.

Rachel's interest in the biography of Fenwick Stonehill was purely selfish. Rachel had heard of Fletch's marriage to the author of the book and that was when she decided to become an actress. Reggie always gave into her whims and this time was no exception. She had counted on Fletch coming to California and sending his wife packing. If this movie was the box office hit she knew it would be, she'd be an overnight sensation and make loads of money. She and Fletch wouldn't need Reggie's money, and they wouldn't have to wait for the old man to die.

For tonight, she'd just settle for the young screenwriter, Grant Walker. Rachel knew Melvin Kessler was looking at her longingly, but he was beginning to bore her. She felt the need for someone young in her life and Grant was an easy target.

She sauntered over to where he was standing. Grant had watched her all evening. Jennifer Reed, the girl he'd left behind in Iowa, was the farthest thing from his mind.

*****

"Look over there, Samantha," said Megan. "Rochelle is headed in for the kill. Poor Grant; he won't know what hit him."

"I'm tempted to go to his rescue," replied Samantha, "but I don't think he'd thank me. He can't take his eyes off the woman. I hope he doesn't do anything foolish and ruin it with his girlfriend Jennifer. Megan, do you think we've stayed long enough? I'm beat; we could sneak out that side door without being noticed."

"I think Brad Taylor would notice," replied Megan. "He's stared at you all evening. Brad is charismatic in his movies, but seeing him in person, he just looks creepy. He's the first movie star I've seen out here and I don't care if I see any others."

"I agree, Megan. I think I've had it for the night. I just want to go back to our suite, call the guys, and go to bed."

*****

While Brad Taylor watched the women exit the room, Reggie Crenshaw didn't miss their escape either.

"Ivor," he called to his bodyguard, "those young women have the right idea; it's time to leave. I think I should save our young writer from Rachel's clutches. Go tell her it's time to go. Carry her out to the car, if necessary before she makes a complete fool of herself."

## CHAPTER 5

After a good night's sleep, Samantha and Megan woke refreshed. The hotel coffee shop was scheduled to open at six o'clock. They were about to leave their suite when the telephone rang.

"Samantha, it's Barry Kline. Melvin has called the cast and crew together this morning. The meeting will be at Seabrook Shores. I thought you and Megan would like to join us. I can swing by the hotel if you're interested."

"Thanks for letting us know, Barry. I'm sure Mr. Kessler won't be happy to see us there, but he can't do much about it if we just show up."

"Marvin takes orders from Mr. C, and I heard the old guy singing your praises last night after you and Megan left."

"Oh, no. I hope Rochelle didn't hear him. She took an instant dislike to me."

"I've had my share of difficult women—men too, for that matter. I'm not looking forward to working with her. Tell me, Samantha, have you had any acting experience?"

"I know you're teasing, Barry, and the answer is no. I'm no competition for Ms. Rochelle Rousseau."

"It's too bad; I think we could have a great movie if we followed your book with you playing the part of Samantha. I'll be by to pick you up in thirty minutes. Will that give you enough time."

"More than enough; we'll wait in the lobby, and thanks, Barry."

*****

"Sounds like they were planning to start without us. I wonder where Grant is. I think he abandoned us in favor of Rochelle. The poor guy; he acted like a love-sick puppy at the party last night."

"Maybe you were right yesterday, Sam, when you thought we should get on the next plane for home. This place is nothing like I thought it would be. I miss Lancashire and I miss Mike."

"Let's give it some thought today. Barry is picking us up soon. If the day is a disaster, we'll be better able to make our decision whether to stay or go. I was looking forward to the guys joining us later. Maybe we can salvage this trip after all."

When Barry held the car door open for Samantha and Megan, Samantha noticed worry lines on Barry's otherwise handsome face. The sleuth in her wanted to hear his personal story. Or was she simply being nosy? Samantha knew it was a little of both.

"Tell us about yourself, Barry; I see you're wearing a wedding ring. Do you have children?"

Barry smiled. "Andie and I have two children, Benjy is five and Chloe is two. I suppose every dad says the same thing, but those two kids are the greatest, I don't know what I'd do without them".

The sadness in his voice didn't escape Samantha's attention.

Barry continued, "Not many people know this, Samantha, but you are easy to talk to. Benjy was diagnosed with leukemia several months ago. It's been a struggle for him, but he's been a trooper through all the treatments." Barry's voice began to tremble slightly.

"Oh, Barry, that's horrible. I'm so sorry for you and your family." Megan expressed her sympathy too.

"He's doing well and he's almost back to his normal, mischievous self. It's been an experience I never want to go through again."

Barry drove his car through the winding road to the Seabrook mansion. The sight of the replica of Stonehill Manor took Samantha's breath away again. Memories of Professor Stonehill and her short-lived stay at Stonehill came back to her. Stonehill Manor was where she'd first met Detective Joseph Fletcher. The circumstances then had been less than ideal for a budding romance, but the attraction was there from their first encounter. He was gruff and suspicious of her. Samantha thought he was the nastiest man she'd ever known, but still, there was an attraction. Who would have guessed that that surly, ill-tempered man was her gentle, loving husband of today?

"This place does something to you, doesn't it, Samantha? Barry asked. "I can see it in your eyes. Hawthorne Stonehill must have done good job duplicating the original mansion."

"It's unbelievable; if it weren't for the palm trees and the ocean behind the building, I would swear I was looking at Stonehill Manor. It's a shame the place is vacant most of the time. I don't understand why Mr. Lambert doesn't sell it. From what Myra Sims has said, he's rarely here."

"I question it too," replied Barry, "I've heard he's a young guy who isn't into lavish parties or a playboy lifestyle; he lives in his London flat and comes to California when his business requires his attention."

"This place must cost a fortune in upkeep. The guy must have money to burn," said Megan.

"Wouldn't that be nice," said Barry wistfully.

Samantha and Megan glanced at each other, both suspecting there was more on Barry's mind than his son's health.

*****

"There you are, Kline," chided a stern Melvin Kessler. "I see you brought those two with you. We have work to

do here and I don't want interference. Do you understand?" He was glaring directly at Samantha.

"You've made it clear you don't wish to listen to ad-
vice on the production of this movie, Mr. Kessler. I must
warn you, I will not allow you to denigrate Professor
Stonehill's name."

"I don't see where you have a choice; you signed over
the rights to your book and I'll do as I please. Let's get
started. Where's Rochelle? She's late. She'd better not be
with that Wagner kid."

"Or what, Melvin?" hissed Rochelle as she walked
through the door. "What business is it of yours who I
spend my time with?"

"Hello, sweetheart; bear with me. I'm tired today, I
didn't get much sleep last night." Melvin whispered in
her ear, "I missed you, baby. Why didn't you call me after the party?"

Rochelle ignored him and instead stared at Samantha,
"What's she doing here?"

"I tried to get rid of her, darlin'; she insists on being
here and I can't throw her out. What's she done to make
you dislike her so?"

"Oh shut up, Melvin; where's Grant? He was supposed to be here this morning. Did you get rid of him instead of her?"

"Grant's making some changes in the script. Why are
you so interested in him, Rochelle? I thought we had
something special together. You know I want to marry
you after the old man kicks."

"Does *something special* have anything to do with the
money I'll inherit after poor Reggie passes?" Rochelle
said as she walked in the opposite direction.

Melvin tried his best to ignore Rochelle's words. He
had a sinking feeling she was becoming disenchanted
with him. He couldn't remember a time when a woman
ended a relationship with him; he was always the first to

break it off. He was all too willing to marry some of them and allowed them to become pregnant. How stupid he'd been to believe them when they said they'd taken precautions. Well, he made sure that would never happen again. The procedure had been a threat to his manhood, but it gave him peace of mind.

Last night when he didn't hear from Rochelle, he was so despondent, he'd placed a bet online. He couldn't afford to make the bet, but it was a sure thing. However, he lost the money and now he was worse off than he was before.

\*\*\*\*\*

Samantha and Megan were fascinated watching Melvin direct the cast. He explained it was simply a run-through and many changes would be made during the production. Grant was re-writing Rochelle's part, so they were starting with the kidnapping.

Brad Taylor played the part of the professor very well. Samantha had to admit he was a good actor although he gave her the creeps. When he was into the part, his focus was on his performance and not on her.

Melinda Sullivan played the part of Victoria Stonehill, now Hill, well too. Samantha thought she resembled the photographs she'd seen of the professor's wife.

Samantha had a difficult time holding back the tears as did Megan.

Melvin approached them and told them if they couldn't control themselves, they could leave.

They were both obstinate enough to stay quiet through the rest of the scene.

\*\*\*\*\*

Grant appeared with copies of the changes he'd made. Melvin looked it over and nodded his head in approval. Melvin handed the revised script to Barry.

"This isn't going to work, Melvin," Barry said upon glancing at the new script. "It's out of character for the professor. Thanks for the effort, Grant, but we won't be making the changes after all."

"Kline, you don't have any say in this," said Melvin. "I'm calling the shots and I say we go with the new script. Melinda, take a break; we'll pick up your scene later. Where's Rochelle? I need her to review the changes."

Joel Young who was playing Detective Fletcher was watching the performance.

"Joel, you're in this scene; go stand by the door to the professor's study. Prop guy, strap the letter opener on Brad's back. I want this to see how it looks."

"Are you directing now, Kessler? If so, you don't need me here," said Barry.

"No, Kline," replied Melvin, "You're the director; I just want to make sure you do your job correctly."

*****

While everyone found their marks, they waited for Rochelle.

Grant sat down next to Samantha. "I'm sorry, Samantha. The new script doesn't resemble your story at all. Kessler had me make drastic changes. Now you're the murderer and hauled off to jail by Fletch's partner. Rochelle is no longer playing the part of you; she turns up as the professor's long-lost daughter, Rachel. The entire show is now all about Rachel and Fletch and their love story."

## CHAPTER 6

Samantha was stunned when she saw a rather plain actress open the door to the set resembling the professor's suite. Brad sat at the professor's desk; he was wearing a gray wig, but didn't look to be in his eighties.

"Good morning, Samantha," he said to the girl. "I called you here today because I will no longer be needing your services. You se, my long-lost daughter has returned. She will be helping me with my memoirs now. So I'm sorry, but I will have to ask you to pack your things and leave."

The girl shouted that the professor couldn't treat her like that after all they'd meant to each other. Brad calmly said he'd never loved her and with that, the actress picked up the letter opener and appeared to stab him in the back.

At that moment, Rochelle opened the door and screamed, "Murderer!" Out of nowhere, Joel Young appeared at the door, threw handcuffs on the girl playing Samantha, and turned her over to his partner. "Fletch" then held a sobbing "Rachel" in his arms and vowed to love her forever.

Samantha began to laugh. "That's ridiculous! Who would believe that nonsense? Have you people even read the story of Professor Stonehill?"

"What's wrong, Samantha? You don't think Fletch could love anyone but an insipid creature like you?" Rochelle asked angrily.

Samantha shrugged off the insult. "Do you know Fletch?" she asked.

"I *know* him in every sense of the word. He and I are lovers; you're a fool if you think he'll stay with you when I'm free and he can have me all to himself."

Samantha knew someone had broken Fletch's heart before they'd met. She remembered a conversation she'd had with his partner, Robin Wells. Robin had said a woman named Rachel had soured him on all women until he met Samantha. Could Rochelle be Rachel? Is that why she seemed to dislike Samantha so much? "Are you Rachel?" asked Samantha.

"Yes, I'm Rachel—the love of Fletch's life. I persuaded Grant to get rid of you in the script and he did it without the violent ending I'd planned, but this way's all right with me as long as you're out of Fletch's life for good."

"Rochelle, no matter how many changes you make to my book, I'm still married to Fletch. If he loved you in the past, he doesn't anymore. I'm his life now."

Reggie Crenshaw walked into the room just after overhearing the conversation between Rachel and Samantha.

"Everyone, go home," he said. "There will be no movie-making today—or any day. Rochelle Rousseau no longer exists. Rachel, Ivor will drive you home. Wait for me there. I have a phone call to make to my attorney and then we'll meet you in my study. I could live with your many liaisons with other lovers, but I refuse to stay married to a woman who professes her love for another man."

"Mr. C," said an anguished Melvin Kessler. "We have a contract. You can't be serious about abandoning the project."

"Melvin, I have contracts with many people. You should have read the small print, but you were too busy bedding my wife. All contracts are null and void. Now, get out of here before I have you arrested for trespassing."

"Reggie, darling!" cried Rochelle, clinging desperately to her husband's sleeve, "you can't believe I'd actually love a cop. I was just acting back there with Samantha. I don't have feelings for anyone but you. Come home with me and I'll show you how much I care for you and only you."

"Get out, Rachel! Ivor, pick her up and carry her. Just get her out of here."

Rachel ran out the front door, shouting for Ivor not to dare touch her, that she had her car and she'd drive herself home. She got in her car and drove it around to the back of the mansion and out of sight of Ivor. She needed time to think; she'd put five years into her marriage and she knew Reggie would leave her without a cent if she couldn't convince him to trust her again. When was the old goat going to die? Maybe she could help his demise along.

*****

Barry wanted to scream; the money he'd been promised would have been enough to pay all Benjy's medical expenses, and avert the foreclosure on his family's home. He should have known this project was too good to be true. Maybe Mr. C would understand and give him at least part of the money he'd contracted for. He had put many hours into the project. The guy couldn't be totally unreasonable, or could he?

*****

Melvin was in agony. Not only was his heart broken when he realized it was over between Rochelle and him, now he was even further in debt than he was yesterday. Now he had to worry about the money he owed for his gambling debt as well as his late alimony and child support payments. He wanted to wring Mr. C's scrawny little neck. He was so close to having everything he wanted. He was sure he could persuade Rachel to marry him after the old codger bit it. Now he was throwing her out of his life because he thought she was in love with some cop from her past. But that cop was married to Samantha Degan, and Melvin doubted he'd be willing to leave his beautiful wife for a trashy woman like Rochelle. He saw Rochelle's car circle the mansion and wondered what she was up to. If she had a plan in mind, he would tell her that a husband couldn't testify against his wife in court. Ah yes, this might work out just fine. He could end up with the girl and the money. He didn't have much time to figure out how to hasten the death of an old man.

*****

"I've been a fool," said Grant Wagner as he waited outside with Samantha and Megan. "I could have ruined everything with Jennifer. I know you warned me about Rochelle, but I didn't listen. I've never known anyone like her before, and I couldn't seem to help myself. I should have known she was only using me to write a script to embarrass you. I'm so sorry I hurt you."

"Grant, you've nothing to be sorry for. You were hired to do a job and that's what you did. I'm sorry for you because you have what it takes to be a meaningful writer and this nonsense wasn't worthy of you. Your first script, although it didn't resemble my book, was well written."

"Thanks, Samantha, you're good for my ego, but this opportunity was my last chance to be a successful writer and now that it's over, I'm ready to go back to Iowa."

"You don't have to give up on your dreams, Grant. Keep writing and working with your dad in his shop. I have no doubt you'll make a name for yourself someday."

"I'll keep that in mind. I left my laptop in the house; I need to go back to get it. I hope we'll see each other again before we leave for home. It's been a pleasure meeting you both." He turned and ran back into the house.

"Samantha, do you think Grant has a talent for writing?" asked Megan. "He's a good guy; I hope Jennifer appreciates him."

"Me too. Here comes Barry; he looks devastated. I thought he'd be happy the project is a bust. I know he didn't like the script even before Rachel made Grant revamp the entire story."

"I'll be just a few minutes," said Barry to the two women. "I want to make sure I didn't leave anything behind in the mansion. It looks like almost everyone has left."

"Take your time, Barry. Megan and I will take a walk by the ocean while we wait for you. It looks like a storm is brewing."

Samantha and Megan took off their shoes and walked in the soft sand. The ocean waves were splashing fiercely against the shore. The rumbling of thunder was heard in the distance.

"It looks like the movie won't be made of the professor's life now. Are you sorry, Sam?"

"Not at all; it's taught me a lesson, and that is to take my time signing a contract in the future. I didn't think it through enough because I was flattered that someone wanted to make a movie of my work. What's that old proverb? *Pride goeth before a fall.* I'll remember that in the future. Not that anyone is going to want to make a movie of my books after this fiasco."

A loud clap of thunder muffled the sound of a scream. The two women quickly rushed back to the house where in the distance they saw Grant in the swimming pool, dragging Mr. C's limp body to the edge. Grant's high school training as a lifeguard was coming in handy. Samantha and Megan watched horrified as Grant struggled to pull Mr. C out of the pool and then as he tried valiantly to breathe air into the man's lungs. But it was too late.

Grant looked up at them with dread. It appeared that Reggie Crenshaw was dead.

## CHAPTER 7

"What are you doing to my husband?" Rachel shouted when she exited the house and saw Grant hovering over Reggie. "You killed him! You killed Reggie!"

Despite the thunder, Samantha and Megan couldn't miss the shrill screams of Rachel Ross. They ran over to the pool deck. Mr. C was lying on his back with his eyes opened wide. Megan muffled a scream herself. Samantha shivered when she saw the look of panic on Grant's face.

"He was in the pool," gasped Grant. "I pulled him out and tried to revive him, but it was too late. I'm so sorry, Rachel. I couldn't help him."

"Why did you kill him, Grant? Why did you kill my sweet husband?" *I'll show them what a magnificent actress I am, I'll show them all,* she thought, and added some heart-wrenching sobs to make her sorrow more authentic.

Samantha reached for her cell phone and dialed 9-1-1 to report what she hoped was an accident.

Barry walked out the patio door, and Samantha noticed a look of horror, but not surprise on his face. She knew Barry was troubled about something other than his son's illness. She liked Barry and could tell he cared deeply for his wife and children.

He was followed by Melvin whose somber face looked gray. He and Rochelle exchanged glances. *If something nefarious had taken place out here,* Samantha thought, *I wouldn't be surprised if those two had something to do with it.*

Samantha noticed a slight pinkish cast to a spot in the water, possibly indicating that Mr. C had bled before he fell into the pool. Samantha remembered the water was too cold for swimming when they were here yesterday. The cold water could have stopped the flow of blood.

"What's going on out here?" Melvin Kessler asked as he strolled around the side of the house. The overbearing man's face was ashen and he looked nervous.

Samantha detected the smell of alcohol on his breath and stepped back. "Mr. Crenshaw is dead."

"I didn't kill him if that's what you're thinking."

"I didn't say anything about murder, did I?" said Samantha. "For all we know, this was an unfortunate accident."

"Whatever," said Kessler. "I'm leaving now. "Anyone want to join me at the pub in the village? We can have a drink to toast Mr. C's demise."

"I think we'd better stay, Mr. Kessler," replied Samantha. "The authorities are on their way; I'm sure they'll have questions for all of us."

"I don't have anything to tell them, I'm leaving," replied Kessler as he patted her on the bottom. She almost turned around and slugged him, but Barry came to her rescue.

"Leave the lady alone, Kessler. You aren't going anywhere. You will wait for the cops along with the rest of us, but do your waiting away from Samantha."

"Thanks, Barry. I was about to slug him before you saved me," said Samantha. "Have you seen Brad Taylor? He must have left before all the excitement. He's a strange man and nothing like he appears on screen. From the little I saw of his performance today, he's a good actor."

"Only mediocre," said Barry, "but better than what's-her-name over there. She's laying it on a little thick. Directing her would have been a challenge. I'm sorry this project turned into such a disaster and I'm sorry for my part in it. I think your book would make a splendid movie. I know a few people who might still be interested. Young Grant has talent too. I know without the restrictions placed on him, he would have done a good job with the screenplay."

"I don't know, Barry," said Samantha, "I'm not sure this whole thing was a good idea. Maybe it's too soon to think about starting over again. I just want to go home and pick up my life where I left it two days ago. I can't believe all that has happened in those two days."

They could hear sirens in the distance. Megan would be happy when the paramedics took the dead body away. She was feeling queasy although she tried to get as far away from Mr. C's body as she could. She looked at the faces of everyone standing helplessly around the body. She knew Grant's dreams had been shattered when the movie was cut short. She hoped he didn't confront Mr. Crenshaw and cause his accident. She had been thrilled when Samantha invited her along on the trip. They'd planned to stay until Mike and Fletch joined them for a vacation. She was sorry Mike wasn't here with her now. She felt a chill and just wished they could go back to the hotel. The sky was dark; the wind was howling, and she could hear the waves crashing to the surf. Samantha came to sit by her side.

"Megan, I've called Fletch. He and Mike are on their way to the airport; they will standby for the earliest flight out here."

"Samantha, you're a mind reader. I was just sitting here wishing Mike was with me."

"I know how you feel. I felt the same way about Fletch. Maybe now you'll know that Mike is the right one for you and make it official. You know how we old married folks are; we want everyone to enjoy the wonderful state of matrimony."

The paramedics walked around the corner of the house followed by two uniformed police officers. While the paramedics examined the body, one police officer asked: "What happened here today?"

"Arrest Grant Wagner; he killed my husband," screeched Rachel, pointing at Grant.

"I didn't kill the man, officer. I walked out the door and saw him face down in the pool. I pulled him out of the water and tried to resuscitate him, but it was too late," replied a distraught Grant.

"Officer, my name is Samantha Degan. I noticed a trace of pink in the water before you arrived. It's not visible now because the filter dissolved it, but if you notice, there a small smear of blood on the patio door. Is it possible the victim was stuck with an object and staggered into the pool?"

"Who might you be, ma'am?" the officer asked.

"I told you, I'm Samantha Degan. I simply told you what I observed."

"The lady's right, Pete," said the other officer. "There is blood smeared on the door."

The medical examiner arrived. Detective Bellamy called him Dr. King. "Whatcha got for me, Doc? Does the guy have a bump on his head?"

"Sure does, Pete. Looks like somebody conked him on the head with a heavy object. I'll need to take him in to perform an autopsy, but I suspect it wasn't the blow that killed him. Sounds like water in his lungs. I'd guess he was knocked daffy and stumbled into the pool. I'll get my full report to you as soon as possible."

"Okay, ladies and gentlemen, I want you to all take a seat. Officer Hendricks will stay here on the patio to make sure you don't talk to each other. I'll question you one at a time. Mr. Wagner, is it? You're first; come with me."

Detective Peter Bellamy entered the study followed by Grant. He closed the door behind them.

Mr. Wagner, why don't you tell me what all you people are doing here in Seabrook Shores. I know an English guy named Lambert owns this place and it's vacant most of the time.

"We were here to prepare for the filming of a movie based on the life of a college professor. Mr. C, that is, Reggie Crenshaw, the dead guy, was financing it. He got mad at his wife and cancelled the whole thing. I came in here to get my computer when I saw Mr. C floating face down in the water. I don't know how long he'd been there, but obviously, it was too late."

"What part did you play in making the movie? Are you an actor?"

"No, sir. I'm a screenwriter; I am responsible for ruining Samantha Degan's excellent biography of an exemplary man and turning it into trash."

"If you felt so strongly, why did you agree to write it?"

"It was my last chance to make it as a writer. It's time to give up my dream. It's all right, though, I hated what I'd done to the story."

"Did Mr. Crenshaw force you to write something you hated?"

"No, he didn't. It was Rochelle Rousseau, Mr. Crenshaw's wife. She's a looker and she led me on and I fell for it. What a jerk."

"Are you the reason Mr. Crenshaw ended production? Was he jealous of your relationship with his wife?"

"No," laughed Grant. "I don't think he noticed. He was mad because he discovered that his wife Rochelle— or Rachel—had a relationship with Samantha Degan's husband before she married him. You see, this was her first acting job and it seems her only interest in the movie was to see the man again."

"Samantha Degan? She's the one who was playing detective out there? What did she have to do with the movie?"

"She wrote the book. Apparently, Rachel saw the book and knew it included parts about her ex, so she decided that filming it would bring the detective out here so she could start up where they left off."

The inside door to the office opened. Ivor looked quizzically at Pete Bellamy. "What's going on here? Where's Mr. Reggie?"

Pete was startled at the presence of the huge man. "Who are you?" he asked.

Ivor's face reddened. "Is Mr. Reggie alright? I didn't want to leave him, but he told me to go watch television while he made some phone calls."

Pete didn't know whether to feel sorry for this oaf of a man or fear him. "Why don't you sit down and tell me your name, fella."

"I'm Ivor; I'm Mr. Reggie's friend, and I help to keep the bad guys away," Ivor said proudly. "I'm going to go find Mr. Reggie now."

"Ivor," Pete Bellamy said gently, "I'm sorry, Mr. Reggie is dead; he drowned in the pool. The paramedics are taking him to the hospital so the doctor can see what made him die. Do you understand, Ivor?"

"No!" Ivor shouted. He bolted out the patio door, calling Reggie's name.

Barry Kline walked over to Ivor and put his hand on his arm gently, urging him to sit down while the paramedics lifted the body bag holding Reggie Crenshaw onto the gurney to take him to the morgue for the autopsy.

It took Barry, Pete, and Officer Hendricks to hold Ivor back. He was sobbing when he looked directly into Barry's eyes. "Murderer!" Ivor shouted.

"Hendricks, have the medics check this guy, will you?" said Detective Bellamy, "I can't question him while he's in this state."

Rachel walked through the door. "Ivor, how did you let this happen? I told Reggie to fire you; you're useless." Rachel turned to the detective, "He's got some kind of sleeping thing going on. He falls asleep just like that," she said, snapping her fingers.

"Are you talking about narcolepsy?" asked Samantha when she heard Rachel's shrill voice. "Narcolepsy is a serious neurological disease if that's what Ivor suffers from; he doesn't deserve to be chastised."

"Shut up, Samantha; no one asked for your opinion."

"She has a point, Mrs. Crenshaw," said the detective. "Suppose you tell me what you've observed about this sleeping pattern."

"The guy's an oaf; Reggie felt sorry for him and hired him as a bodyguard. He would never hurt anyone. Reggie always said he just had to look at a person and they'd back off. Reggie had a sixth sense about Ivor and his sleeping problem. He knew when the dope was going to drop off. He'd tell him to go watch television and Ivor did it. A few minutes later, he'd be snoring away. I think he's just lazy."

"Ivor," asked Detective Bellamy, "did Mr. Crenshaw tell you to watch television this evening?"

"Yes," replied Ivor. "I watched *Lucy;* she's so funny. I don't know what she was doing, but everyone was laughing."

"Were you sleeping, Ivor?"

"Yes, sir; Mr. Reggie says I should sleep when I get sleepy."

Ivor began to cry again at the mention of Reggie's name. The paramedic came to walk him to the sofa in the living room where he took his vitals.

"I wonder what will happen to the poor man?" said Samantha, not expecting an answer to her question.

"I don't care where he stays, but it won't be with me," said Rachel. "He's creepy and I won't have him in my house."

Megan rolled her eyes. *What had Fletch ever seen in this self-centered woman?* she thought. Her cell phone sounded and Megan was happy to hear Mike's voice. He told her he and Fletch were at the airport. Fletch was renting a car and they would be at the hotel soon.

"No, Mike, something terrible has happened! A man has died at the mansion at Seabrook Shores. The police are here questioning everyone. I don't know how long it will be before we can leave. Do you think you and Fletch can find your way here? I'll ask Grant Wagner to give you directions."

"No, we can find it. What's the address? Fletch and I both felt uneasy about this movie deal. We'll be there as soon as we can."

Megan gave him the address and told Samantha the guys were on their way. Both women were relieved.

## CHAPTER 8

Although the freeway was packed with cars, Fletch managed to find his way to the turn-off for Seabrook Shores. Driving a patrol car on the streets of Chicago all those years had finally paid off.

Driving up the road to the mansion, Fletch was amazed that the house looked identical to Stonehill Manor.

A police officer stopped the car and asked for identification. The officer called Detective Bellamy to ask permission for Detective Fletcher and Mike Thompson to be allowed on the premises.

"Detective Fletcher is here," said Detective Bellamy, turning to Samantha. "I assume he's the sleuth's husband."

Samantha nodded her head yes. It was Rachel who yelled: Fletch is here! I have to see him!" She ran out the front door and down the driveway before anyone could stop her.

"This is turning into a very interesting case," said Bellamy to his partner. "Isn't she the one who was weeping over her dead husband a few minutes ago? Now she's running after a guy who's married to Jessica Fletcher here?"

"It's Samantha Degan Fletcher; Jessica was a much older woman," Samantha replied.

*****

Fletch saw a woman running toward the car, and as she got closer, he thought she looked familiar.

"Fletch, darling! I'm so glad you're here. Reggie is dead; I'm free!" she said excitedly.

"Rachel, what are you doing here? Where's my wife?"

"It doesn't matter where that silly girl is; the important thing is that we can be together again. Oh, Fletch, I've missed you so." Rachel opened the door to his rental car and wrapped her arms around his neck.

Fletch struggled to get out of the car and out of Rachel's clutches. He saw Samantha hurrying down the path, so he pushed Rachel aside and greeted his wife with a hug. "What's happened, Sam? I don't understand any of this. What's Rachel Ross doing here and who died?"

Samantha explained that Rachel had talked her husband, Reggie Crenshaw, into buying the rights to Professor Stonehill's memoirs, and that she had planned to star in the movie, calling herself Rochelle Rousseau. She explained that Reggie always did as his wife asked, but he called off the movie when he realized that the only reason she wanted to act in this film was so she could get together with Fletch again.

"Is the woman cracked? Why would she think I'm interested in her after all these years? Did she know you're my wife? I thank my lucky stars she dumped me because if she hadn't, I'd would be living in Chicago and I'd never have met you." Fletch held Samantha close while a furious Rachel looked on.

"You have to admit, she is beautiful," sighed Samantha.

"Not as beautiful as my wife," Fletch said. "I see she's added some enhancements since I knew her—not that I noticed," he said with a chuckle.

"Of course, you noticed; they're hard to miss," giggled Samantha. "She's glaring at us; let's go inside. I'm sure Megan is getting impatient wait for Mike. Detective Bellamy let me come out here after Rachel dashed away. I annoy him, but he must believe in the sanctity of marriage because he told me to come out and rescue my husband."

Pete Bellamy shook hands with Fletch. "I've lost control of this investigation," he said. "Your wife's observant, isn't she? I suspect she'll solve this case long before I've finished interrogating these folks."

"Did she tell you she writes mystery novels? Looking for clues is second nature to her. Tell me what you've got? I'll help, if I can."

"What I've got is a dead man. His body was found floating face down in the pool. The young writer, Grant Wagner, pulled the body from the pool and attempted to resuscitate him. The paramedics found a gash in his head that might not have killed him, but at least caused him to lose his balance. It's assumed he fell into the pool where the cold water stopped the bleeding. Samantha figured that out; I can't take credit for the theory, but I do believe it's possible. There's smeared blood on the patio door; the victim might have touched his bleeding head before he opened the door."

"The victim, Reggie Crenshaw," Detective Bellamy continued, "was footing the bill for the film production of your wife's novel. Apparently, he balked when it was obvious his wife, Rachel, had taken it upon herself to revamp the plot to feature her and her detective lover. Then, he terminated his backing and told everyone to get out.

"The department has reported their findings while running preliminary background checks. The screenwriter, Grant Wagner, is broke; this film was his last chance at fame before giving up and returning to his hometown in Iowa.

"Barry Kline is a family man. He lives with his wife and two kids in an upscale neighborhood in the suburbs. His young son was recently diagnosed with leukemia; the kid's doing well, but the expense of his treatments nearly wiped him out financially. Directing this movie was his only hope of avoiding foreclosure on the family home.

"Melvin Kessler, the producer, has been having an ongoing affair with the dead man's wife. Crenshaw knew about it and about involvements she's had with other men and looked the other way. You, however, were a different story. He felt threatened by her feelings for you, Detective. Melvin is drowning in debt thanks to ex-wives and children from those marriages. He attempted to solve his financial problems betting on a *sure* thing and now he's worse off than before. He needed the money his share of profits from the movie would have brought.

"Brad Taylor's better days as an actor are behind him. But you can't call him a *has been* just yet. His career would be given a much-needed shot in the arm by playing a sophisticated older gentleman in the movie. He was in trouble with the law a few years ago when he stalked an ingénue he'd met at a party. She eventually issued a restraining order and after a confrontation with the girl's boyfriend that ended with Taylor in a coma, the girl and her boyfriend moved back to their hometown."

"How did you get this information in such a short time?" asked Fletch.

"It's not difficult in this town. People are more than willing to share information. Our biggest problem is we have to make sure the details aren't a fabrication of events." The detective continued.

"Rachel Ross is a party girl. She married Reggie Crenshaw for his money and he knew it. Reggie was heard telling Rachel he'd had enough; he was throwing her out of his home and leaving her penniless. Of course, this being a community property state, he was obligated to share his wealth with his wife. However, there is speculation that he and Rachel were never legally married. Reggie has a wife and daughter living in Santa Monica. He has systematically transferred his funds to the daughter and only draws from an account in her name as he needs funds. Thus, Rachel's inheritance is minimal; she doesn't know this, and I feel sorry for the poor sap who tells her she's a pauper."

"Are you saying Rachel is a suspect?" asked Fletch. "She could have killed Reggie expecting to be a wealthy widow and it turns out she isn't a widow or wealthy after all? After a certain amount of time living together, wouldn't the relationship be considered a common-law marriage in California?"

"That's a possibility, but it doesn't change the fact that over the last five years, Reggie has relinquished his wealth to his daughter, Regina Crenshaw. She's been told of her father's death and wants to meet with me. She should be here in about twenty minutes," said Detective Bellamy.

"Did Rachel know about his wife and daughter before her so-called marriage? I had the impression when Rachel told me she was marrying this Reggie Crenshaw, she thought he was a confirmed bachelor," said Fletch.

"I don't think she knows about the wife or the daughter, and definitely not about the money. I don't know how word got out regarding Reggie's death. Maybe one of the neighbors saw the ambulance and police cars and called the television station because reporters have begun showing up. The officers are holding them back, but it won't be long before we're forced to give them something to report. This investigation is only going to get worse. Reggie's lawyer heard the news and is on his way. He wants Rachel Ross held for questioning before she returns to the home she shared with Reggie. He knows she will explode when she finds out there's no money for her."

*****

Gina Crenshaw drove her two-year-old BMW coupe along the freeway to the turn-off for Seabrook Shores.

The car was one of the few extravagances Gina had allowed herself to buy. She was paying it off in installments even though her father's money was available to her.

Regina Alexandra Crenshaw was named after both her parents. Her mother called her Gina from the time she was an infant and most people were not aware her given name was the female version of Reginald.

Gina's mother, Alexandra, had met Reggie Crenshaw when she was barely out of her teens. Although her family lived comfortably on the outskirts of Los Angeles, they were far from wealthy. After her college graduation, Alex and three of her friends flew to Maui for their last carefree vacation before settling down in jobs. On their first night on the island, they met young men who told them of a party they'd planned to crash. After a few piña coladas, the girls decided to join them.

The young people were soon discovered and asked to leave, but not before Reggie Crenshaw spotted the young woman with long blonde hair and a golden tan on her slim body. He invited the group to stay as his guest. Reggie was several years older than Alexandra, but the years seemed to fade away as they spoke. Alex had never met a man as charming as Reggie, and Reggie was attracted to the innocence he found in Alexandra. The couple had a whirlwind courtship and Reggie, who never believed in marriage, proposed the last night of Alexandra's vacation. Alexandra accepted and before she could change her mind, Reggie whisked her off to Paris on his jet where they were married.

For the next six months, Reggie doted on his bride. They traveled the world; Alexandra saw places and things she'd only read about. It was exhilarating for a while, but Alexandra wondered if they'd ever settle down. She suspected she was going to have a baby, but wanted to be sure before she mentioned it to Reggie.

"Reggie," she said on one of the rare evenings they dined alone, "I have loved traveling, but I miss seeing my family. Do you think we could go back to California and look for a house?"

"Alexandra, dearest, I've never owned a house in my life, but if that's what you want, that's what we'll do."

Before the week ended, they were on Reggie's jet headed home. Alexandra had a wonderful reunion with her parents and sister. Reggie put on the charm but didn't win over Alexandra's father. He didn't approve of the marriage before he'd met Reggie and meeting him only increased his disapproval.

Alexandra found a house near her parents' home. It never occurred to Reggie that he would live in a mundane house in a mundane neighbor. What good would all his wealth do if he was stuck in suburbia? He would be miles away from the parties and the nightlife. He longed for the days when he stayed up until dawn and slept the day away only to start all over again the next night.

Reggie planned to have a talk with Alex and convince her this was not the life for them when she told him she was pregnant with his baby. It never entered Reggie's mind that he would ever be a father. The more he thought about it though, the better he liked the idea of a son and heir to carry on the Crenshaw name. All through Alexandra's pregnancy, he stayed by her. Alexandra couldn't convince him her condition was normal and she didn't need a nurse and doctor at her beck and call.

To Reggie's dismay, Alexandra insisted the baby be born in a hospital. He protested but gave in to her wishes. He never considered the possibility his child would be a girl. The disappointment showed in his eyes when he greeted his wife and daughter after the birth.

"I'm sorry she's a girl, Reggie, but look at her beautiful face. I know you'll learn to love her as much as I do."

Reggie took one look at the sleeping baby and his heart felt like it would burst with pride. Alexandra told him Regina was a mouthful for a tiny baby. "We'll call her Gina for short."

Little Gina was the apple of her father's eye. For the next six months, he settled in to his fatherhood role. He and Alexandra went to parties on the weekends but were home before midnight to check on their precious baby. Reggie lost touch with many of his friends and found he had nothing to do all day. He loved his wife and baby, but he was restless. Alexandra could sense he was bored.

"Have you ever thought of getting a job, Reggie?" she asked.

"What kind of job would you suggest, Alexandra?" Reggie replied. "I wouldn't qualify for flipping hamburgers; I've never worked a day in my life."

"Reggie, you have charm. You could be a salesman or a tour guide. That's an idea. How about a volunteer at the visitor's center? You enjoy talking to people."

"Do you honestly expect me to chat with tourists? Don't be ridiculous, Alexandra."

"Well, you have to do something; you're underfoot all day long. Your only interest is being with Gina; you're spoiling her, Reggie. She is still a baby and can't learn to entertain herself with you hovering around her all the time."

"You're right, Alexandra. I need to get out of this house and this town. I'll hire two nannies, if need be, and we'll go to Paris. Gina will be well taken care of and we'll be there in time for the social season."

"No, Reggie, I won't live that life again. It's obvious you aren't happy with me and Gina. I won't stand in your way if you want a divorce."

"Who said anything about a divorce? I love you, Alexandra, but I'm not a man who can be idle for long. I have been a part of the social scene for as long as I can remember. I wish you'd agree to go with me to Paris, but I'll go alone if you can't tear yourself away from your family."

That was how Reggie and Alexandra's love story ended. Reggie went off to Paris and Alexandra stayed home with her baby. She was sad that her fairytale had ended, but also relieved that Reggie wasn't moping around the house all day. Reggie was generous in paying Alexandra and Gina's living expenses and never expected Alexandra to work for a living. Alexandra, however, knew she wanted to be useful and worked as a school secretary when Gina began kindergarten.

The subject of divorce never came up. Reggie visited California every few months. Gina loved her father and was always happy to see him. Alexandra's life revolved around her daughter. She never had any desire to date and therefore, didn't ask Reggie for a divorce.

Reggie had plenty of women through the years. He never took any of his flings seriously and left a few broken hearts along the way. When Rachel Ross came into his life, it was different. She was beautiful and intelligent, a combination Reggie didn't often find in the women he dated. He knew she was involved romantically with a cop and feared she'd leave Reggie for the other guy. He had no desire to end his marriage to Alexandra and suspected Rachel was more attracted to his money than to him. He asked her to marry him and she agreed. He didn't let her know he was already married and arranged for a fake ceremony. His lawyer cautioned Reggie that he would be wise to funnel his money to his daughter as a safeguard against Rachel ending up with half his estate.

Gina had no idea how much her father was worth until he started to unload his money into a trust for her. He arranged to have a draw of the funds for his living expenses. She and her mother had lived comfortably, but not extravagantly. Gina was happy with her life and had no wish to live the life her father seemed to enjoy. She knew he was with a woman named Rachel and suspected Rachel didn't know he was still married to her mother. The police officer who called her said the cause of her father's death was being investigated. She wondered if Rachel had had something to do with it.

## CHAPTER 9

"Detective Bellamy, Gina Crenshaw is here, I had her take a seat in the parlor."

"Thanks, Will," Pete said and asked Fletch if he'd like to meet her too.

Gina was a very pretty young woman who looked like the typical California girl with her long blonde hair and tanned slim body. Pete Bellamy suspected she looked like her mother, as she bore no resemblance to the man who lay dead on the patio several hours before.

"Ms. Crenshaw, I'm Detective Bellamy and this is Detective Fletcher. Detective Fletcher is here as a consultant. With your permission, he will sit in on our conversation. We are both very sorry for your loss, ma'am."

"Thank you, Detective. I have no objection to Detective Fletcher's being here. I don't have anything to offer. I was hoping you could give me some answers."

"I wish I could tell you more, ma'am; the coroner's report hasn't arrived yet. We have reason to believe your father suffered a blow to the head. He may have been stunned by the injury and stumbled into the pool. CPR was performed, but it was apparently too late."

"Is Rachel Ross a suspect? I saw her car out front. Did she discover her marriage to my father was a fake? I know his behavior is despicable, but he *is* my father and I cared about him." Gina's chin trembled, but she managed to regain her composure. Now was not the time to break down; she wanted answers and had to control her emotions while she waited to hear what the detective had to say.

"Are you all right, Gina?" asked Fletch. "My wife's in the other room; she can be very compassionate; would you like me to call her?"

"I'm fine, Detective Fletcher. Was your wife here when Father died? Maybe she has the answers I'm looking for."

*****

Samantha joined them in the parlor; she offered her condolence to Gina. Samantha could see a slight resemblance to Reggie Crenshaw in the young woman, but guessed she looked more like her mother. Samantha answered Gina's questions about why her father was in the mansion and explained the situation with the movie that would never be.

Gina felt comfortable with Samantha and began to open up about the financial arrangement she'd had with her father. Reggie had confided in his daughter before his charade of a wedding to Rachel that a part of him would always love Alexandra, but he needed the companionship of a wife.

"Rachel is a beautiful woman and much younger than I am, Gina. I'm not a fool. I know my wealth is what attracts her to me. Her devotion to me will always be in question; therefore, I'm arranging to have my assets turned over to you. I will draw from an account set up for living expenses. The marriage is not legal and her share of my assets will be minimal. She doesn't know about you or your mother and I'd like to keep it that way."

"Father, believe it or not, I like the world I live in. I don't want your money. Why don't you give it to Mom instead?"

"Gina, your mother would never accept it. She refuses to take any of my money for herself. She doesn't begrudge my helping you out, but she's supported herself for many years."

Gina's lifestyle hadn't changed since she became a wealthy woman. She let the accountants handle her holdings and only requested money for charities she felt were worthy of donations. She'd attended a local college and had recently accepted a job in the human resources department of a local hospital.

\*\*\*\*\*

"Samantha, you're the writer Samantha Degan. I didn't make the connection at first. I've read your book and it was fascinating. It's too bad Rachel was involved and made changes; it would have made a wonderful movie the way you wrote it."

Fletch smiled with pride at the kind words about his wife's writing. He knew she was a special person and it was nice to hear others say it too.

"Detectives, I'm not sure I want to be here when Rachel finds out she's not the wealthy widow she believes she is. I think Father was cruel not to leave her anything after five years of living with him. I'll see what can be done to arrange a financial settlement with her."

\*\*\*\*\*

Meanwhile, in the study, Officer Hendricks was having a difficult time controlling Rachel. He was tempted to handcuff her to a chair, but knew that might end his career as a cop.

"I'm a wealthy widow now and I will not stand for this treatment. My husband has been murdered and I need the sympathy of my dear friend, Fletch."

"Ma'am, I've been instructed to hold you here while waiting for Mr. Crenshaw's lawyer to arrive. You're getting yourself all worked up and it's not necessary. 'Please sit down and try to stay calm."

"Oh shut up! Where is Grant Wagner? He's the one who killed my dear Reggie. I hope he's on his way to prison right now".

Melvin Kessler watched from across the room. He longed to take Rachel, the now wealthy widow, in his arms. Her beautiful face was distorted in anger and her voice was shrill, but it didn't dampen her appeal. He wondered about the guy they called Fletch. He's married to Samantha and she's pretty hot stuff herself. *Surely, I don't have anything to fear from him,* he thought. *He and Rachel are old friends and that's all there is to it. I'm sure when we get out of here, Rachel will come running to me. Her husband is dead and she has to make a show of being the grieving widow.*

Barry Kline sat watching Grant Wagner. He didn't think the kid intended to kill Crenshaw if he did conk him over the head. The old man surprised everyone when he abruptly stopped the film. Barry was sorry he hadn't followed his initial instincts and turned the job down. Of course, he couldn't do that with all those bills waiting to be paid. He wanted to call Andie, but what would he say? Some big oaf named Ivor had called him a murderer. As if things weren't bad enough; now he could very well be held on suspicion of murder.

Megan Fairchild and Mike Thompson were allowed to walk around the grounds. Megan had been questioned and was not considered a suspect in the case.

"I wish I knew why Samantha was called to the parlor with Fletch and Detective Bellamy. I can't imagine who this mysterious person is they're interviewing," said Megan.

"This whole thing has me baffled. I'm sorry you and Samantha were involved in the mess. Fletch said the film was not a chronicle of Samantha's book after all."

"No, Mike, what began as a fairytale has turned into a disaster. The revised screenplay had little to do with actual events and became a love story between Rachel and Fletch. It was disgusting."

"Rachel doesn't seem to be Fletch's type at all. He was genuinely surprised to see her and not in a good way. She's the opposite of Samantha. And what's with that Brad Taylor character? He can't seem to take his eyes off Samantha."

"Isn't he creepy? Don't you remember him in *Parker's Way*? We saw that old movie last month on television. He was so handsome in the film. The makeup artist they used in the movie should win an award."

*****

Brad Taylor was happy the Fairchild woman and her boyfriend weren't in the room. He knew she'd been looking suspiciously at him when he watched Samantha. He couldn't stop himself; she was beautiful and he pictured them being together for the rest of their lives. Nobody knew what he had discovered about the mansion. He knew many of these old places had secret passageways and he was determined to find one in this place. In the movies, the passage was always behind a bookshelf and there were plenty of those in the study. He felt along the side of every row of books until he touched a button. He pushed it and a door opened. He was happy he'd remembered to bring a flashlight. He closed the door behind him and walked carefully into the room. There was an over-stuffed chair and an ottoman with an end table and lamp beside it. The furniture was dusty but inviting. He imagined that once the butler used this room as his private get-a-way. He saw an empty decanter off to the side. He guessed that at one time, the butler had filled the decanter with his employer's brandy and read in the peace and quiet of his hide-a-way. *This is the perfect place*, he thought to himself.

He hoped no one saw him when he disappeared into this sanctuary. He was in this safe place when he heard Mr. Crenshaw enter the study. What would he do if he was discovered? His plan would be ruined and the old man would get Ivor to remove him bodily from the premises. He was distraught when he realized he'd left the bookcase slightly ajar. Someone else was in the room; he heard voices, but he was too upset to understand what was being said. He let his mind drift into a happier place and tried to block out the noises from outside. Someone was yelling. Were they yelling at him? He didn't know. He closed his eyes to make the images go away. He thought of Samantha and the happy times they would have together. He would forget about what had happened in the study and think only of Samantha with the golden hair.

Later, he slid out of his hiding place and took a handkerchief out of his pocket and wiped the surfaces of the bookcase and left the room through the inside door. He didn't think anyone saw him, but he wasn't sure.

Now, sitting in this room with all these people, he wondered if he was the prime suspect and knew he had to give the cops a plausible explanation as to why he was still in the mansion after he—and everyone else—had been asked to leave.

## CHAPTER 10

Blake Lambert settled back in his first-class seat on the airplane, sipping a brandy and hoping it would put him to sleep. It would be morning in Los Angeles before he arrived. He was only twenty-seven, but he felt middle-aged. All this transcontinental traveling was making him an old man before his time. He'd been thinking seriously of closing his London office and moving his entire operation to Los Angeles. He knew California had gotten a bad rap, but he liked the casual lifestyle of the western United States. He never felt comfortable in the mansion in Seabrook Shores. He'd bought the place because of the stories his grandmother had told him about it. The place never lived up to Grandmother's imagination and he felt the walls closing in on him when he was there. Now, a man had died on the estate and under suspicious circumstances. *Why didn't I put it up for sale a year ago?* he thought. *It would be someone else's headache now. I don't know what possessed me to agree to have that stupid movie filmed there. It was because of Professor Stonehill's father that Grandmother's heart was broken almost a century ago.*

*****

Wilson Hines arrived at the front door of the mansion in Seabrook Shores. He was familiar with the exclusive area due to his wealthy client list. Wilson was a widower and in demand when a hostess needed an extra at her dining room table. Wilson had received his law degree, passed the California bar and worked as a clerk for Judge Hamilton Reynolds. Judge Reynolds was the father of Olivia Reynolds. His only child was the apple of her father's eye. Her mother was a beauty but Olivia was the image of her father. Although Hamilton was an attractive man, his features were not complimentary to his rather homely daughter.

Wilson had turned on the charm and had won the heart of Olivia Reynolds. In Olivia's heart, she knew she wasn't the love of Wilson's life, but she thought she loved enough for both of them. Their marriage was satisfactory. Although Wilson never felt great passion for his wife, he was comfortable in the marriage.

It was a stormy night when Olivia and Wilson met her parents for dinner at the country club. The son of a client had been arrested for a traffic violation and the client had called Wilson to meet him at the local precinct.

Wilson had left the family gathering after Hamilton had said he would drive Olivia home. He gave her a kiss on the cheek and that was the last time he'd seen her alive.

On the way to Olivia's home, a car came out of nowhere and struck Hamilton's car head-on. The driver of the other car and all the occupants of Hamilton's car were killed instantly.

Although saddened by the loss of his wife, Wilson found he enjoyed living alone without anyone to answer to. His client list grew and he was considered one of the most eligible bachelors in the city. He had no desire to marry again and agreed to attend dinner parties mainly because he could meet rich people who might eventually become his clients.

It was at one of those dinner parties that he met Reggie Crenshaw. Reggie pulled him off to the corner and told him he wanted to marry without divorcing his current wife.

"Mr. Crenshaw, that is bigamy and against the law."

"I know that, Hines. I didn't say I wanted the marriage to be legal. I want the bride to think it's a real marriage.

Confidentially, I don't trust her; she has feelings for a cop in Chicago, but she wants what only I can give her with my excessive wealth."

"The legality of such an arrangement is questionable. Why not just ask her to live with you? Either that or divorce your wife. What kind of hold does the woman have on you?"

"I won't divorce my wife; I love her and my daughter. Unless Alexandra wants to marry again, we will remain legally married. As far as Rachel living with me, she will only accept having a ring on her finger before she'll agree to that arrangement."

"If you do follow through with this, there's nothing to keep Rachel from taking a good share of your money if the relationship falls through. This is a community property state and a judge would not look kindly on the type of deception you are suggesting."

"I've thought of that, Hines. That's why I want to transfer all my assets to my daughter, Regina. I will, of course, be able to draw from the accounts for my living expenses. I plan to give Rachel everything she could ask for to keep her with me for several years to come. I can tolerate anything she might do except continuing her relationship with that cop."

Wilson had failed to persuade Reggie to abandon his plan; the man was determined to follow through. Now it was Wilson who was going to have to break the news to Rachel Ross that she was not entitled to any of Reggie's money.

"Hello, officer. I'd like to speak with my client's wife in private, if I may."

"Of course, sir. The den isn't occupied; you won't be disturbed in there."

"Rachel, I'm sorry for your loss," Wilson said. "Will you follow me? We have some business to discuss."

"Hello, Wilson. This is a very sad time for me," Rachel said, unconvincingly. "I understand Reggie's estate must be settled promptly without delay. I'll sign whatever papers you need to transfer Reggie's funds to my name."

Wilson could feel the perspiration forming on his forehead as she spoke. This was not going to be an easy task.

Rachel tried to act the part of the somber widow, but it wasn't easy with her heart pounding in her chest. When she'd married Reggie, she thought she might have to put up with him for a year or two, but never imagined he would live for another five years. He'd never done a lick of work in his life and she supposed that was why his heart had been so strong. If it took a pop on the back of his head to end his pampered life, so be it. She was a wealthy woman now. Even if she was accused of murder, she had enough money to pay for all the defense lawyers in the country.

Rachel sat down on the sofa in the den while the sun cast a warmth in the otherwise cold, stark room. She looked into Wilson Hines' eyes and thought she saw fear in them. She listened while he read from a statement prepared by Reggie before his death. The last thing she heard was Wilson's voice telling her she would be paid one thousand dollars and given enough money for plane fare back to her hometown of Chicago.

The dead silence was followed by one single word, "No!" she roared loud enough to be heard throughout the first floor of the mansion.

"I have an idea Rachel has just been told of her financial situation," said Gina. "I know she was a user and took advantage of my father, but he deceived her too. She deserves to have some money and I'd like to make sure she's taken care of until she can resume her life again."

Rachel burst into the room. "Where's this so-called daughter? I want a paternity test. I don't know what your

racket is, lady. Detective, I want her arrested for fraud."
Rachel saw Fletch standing by the window and ran to him
sobbing.

"Rachel, get a hold of yourself. Reggie's daughter is
his legitimate heir; she's willing to offer you enough
money to get you back on your feet. I wouldn't alienate
her if I were you."

"Fletch, I'm not a married woman; we could have
been together all these years. We'll make up for lost time
now."

"Rachel, did you forget I have a wife?" He gently
pushed her away and went to Samantha's side.

"You'll divorce her and we'll be together. I have always loved you, Fletch."

"Rachel, pull yourself together. You don't love me
and, what's more, I don't love you. Samantha and I will
leave you to answer questions for Detective Bellamy. I
suggest you answer him truthfully."

When Fletch and the others left Rachel alone with Pete
Bellamy, she sneered at the closed door. Pete couldn't
make out the words she mumbled, but thought he detected a threat to Samantha Degan.

"Ms. Ross," he said, not knowing what name to call
her under the circumstances, "tell me what happened this
afternoon after Mr. Crenshaw stopped work on the movie."

"I can't possibly talk to you now, Detective. I'm a
grieving widow and need time alone."

"If you don't feel up to it, we can continue our discus-
sion at the police station in the morning. Officer Hendricks will arrange for a patrol car to pick you up at eight
o'clock tomorrow morning."

"That won't be necessary," she acquiesced. "I'd gotten
in my car and started to leave when I realized I'd left my
makeup case behind. I parked in the back of the house so
Ivor wouldn't see me. Reggie told him to escort me home

but I didn't want to be alone with the big lug. He hates me, you know. Anyway, I snuck in through the back door and that's when I saw Grant Wagner strangling my dear Reggie." The tears streamed down her cheeks as she spoke.

"Did you see Mr. Wagner's hands around Mr. Crenshaw's neck?"

"Well, no, by the time I saw him, he was pushing on Reggie's chest. I think he was trying to crush Reggie's ribs or something. Grant had told me this movie was his last chance and Reggie took away his dream."

"Do you think it's possible Grant was administering CPR to Reggie?"

"Oh, I don't know. I don't know anything about that stuff. I'm just telling you what I saw and that was Grant killing my husband."

"Tell me what you know about Melvin Kessler. What was your relationship with Mr. Kessler?"

"Melvin is in love with me," Rachel grinned. "Reggie wasn't always up to the task if you know what I mean. I am a woman of passion and Melvin was often available. Of course, I never had any real feelings for him; he was simply a diversion."

"You say Melvin was in love with you. Did he ask you to leave Reggie to be with him?"

"Oh, heavens no. Melvin wasn't in a position to support another wife. I had him investigated, he has ex-wives and children who are draining him financially. Between you and me, his gambling is out of hand too. I heard him on the phone earlier and it sounded like his bookie was giving him some bad news about a horse he'd bet on. This job would have saved him. He didn't know it, but I was ending our relationship. I wanted to free myself up for Fletch, you see."

"Detective Fletcher is a married man; did you expect him to leave his wife for you?"

"I'm married too, at least I thought I was," she frowned. "I'm sure he would dump that little twit to be with me and now that I'm free, that's exactly what he will do."

"I wouldn't count on it, Ms. Crenshaw."

Pete didn't think much of Rachel Ross, but didn't think she had murdered Reggie Crenshaw. He told her he was finished questioning her, but she shouldn't leave town. Rachel told the detective the lawyer said she had thirty days to vacate the penthouse apartment she'd shared with Reggie. *That gave her thirty days to find another sucker*, Pete thought to himself.

Pete called Barry Kline into the room next. Fletch rejoined him and Barry asked that Samantha be in the room too. He trusted her not to rush to judgment. His family life depended on him giving the right answers to Detective Bellamy's questions.

"Mr. Kline," the detective began, "why don't you tell us your activities between the time Mr. Crenshaw announced he was ending the project and he was dead on the patio floor."

"Mr. Crenshaw told everyone to leave the premises. I'm sorry I didn't follow his directions. I wanted to talk with Grant Wagner and Samantha about the possibility of presenting the original version of the professor's story to some of the folks in the legitimate movie studios."

"When I was approached about doing this project, I read Samantha's book and felt it was an extremely worthy undertaking. I was happy for the opportunity both professionally and financially, and signed a contract in haste. When I saw what was being done to the original story, it made my skin crawl. Samantha and Grant are both very gifted writers and I thought together the three of us could salvage the story."

"Mr. Kline," said Pete, "sometimes I wish I'd chosen another profession and this is one of those times. Isn't it

true you have amassed a substantial amount of debt because of your son's medical bills?"

"Yes, sir, it's true. My son is now well on the road to a
full recovery. This job would have given our family the
income to pay the bills and continue the payments on our
home. I admit, I was upset when Mr. Crenshaw made that
impossible for me, but I assure you, I wouldn't—and
didn't—kill him because of it."

Samantha smiled at Barry sympathetically; he was a
good and decent man and she didn't believe for one minute that he'd caused harm to Mr. Crenshaw.

"Mr. Kline," Pete continued, "I'm happy to hear your
son is well again. I don't have more questions for you
today and you're free to go home to your wife and children. I'll be contacting you if I need more information."

Melvin Kessler was called in next.

"How much longer do I have to hang around this
dump?" He tried to hide his shaking hands.

"Do you have someplace better to be?" asked Pete,
guessing the man would head straight to a bar.

"Let's get it over with. I didn't kill the old goat. Maybe I had reason to, but I didn't do it. Tell me, is it true
Rachel was never legally married to Crenshaw?"

Pete ignored his question. "What reason did you have
to kill Mr. Crenshaw, Melvin?"

"He promised me this job and then he pulled it out
from under me. He was a vindictive old man and was
jealous because his so-called wife was in love with me."

"Why didn't you leave the mansion when he told everyone to go?" asked Pete.

"I was looking for Rachel; I saw her drive around to
the back of the house and I wanted her to go have a drink
with me. I know this place is dry as a bone because I've
been searching everywhere for a bottle. I'm not fussy; I'll
drink anything. This Lambert guy must be a real winner;

there isn't a jug in the whole place, even in the wine cellar."

"According to Ms. Ross, she came in through the back door by the pool. How could you miss her if you saw her car pull behind the house?"

"My eyesight isn't so good. Is that a crime, Detective?"

"No, sir, but murder is and I think you had motive and opportunity."

"I'm not sayin' another word until my lawyer gets here."

"That's your right, Mr. Kessler; we'll wait for your lawyer before we finish questioning you. Have a seat in the other room, please."

"Now wait just a minute. Are you telling me I can't leave here until you finish questioning me? What if my lawyer can't get here until tomorrow? You can't hold me here."

"You're right, sir. However, I can hold you in the county jail overnight until your attorney arrives. This is a murder investigation and you, along with others, are suspects."

"Okay, ask away; I have to get home to feed my sick cat," Melvin lied.

Detective Bellamy questioned him for another ten minutes. He believed the man was more intent on getting his alcohol fix than murdering an old man. Finally, he told Melvin he was free to go, but not to leave town and not to drive drunk. Melvin looked at the detective in surprise. How did the man know he was in dire need of a drink?

Brad Taylor was nervous when he entered the room for questioning next. Why was Samantha sitting in the room with that man they called Fletch? He longed to touch her hair and her face. She looked uncomfortable when she glanced his way. Was this her way of telling him she needed to be rescued? He would answer the detective's questions, but he wouldn't tell him what he remembered. He wouldn't tell anyone except Samantha.

"Mr. Taylor, where were you when Mr. Crenshaw was discovered floating in the pool?"

"I was in the library; I find I need to wind down after a performance. The sofa in that room is very comfortable."

"It's my understanding there wasn't any kind of performing today. The crew was setting up and waiting for script changes."

"That's true, Detective. You wouldn't understand; I'm an artist and I'm always in the performance mode."

Detective Bellamy and Fletch both noticed Brad Taylor looking longingly at Samantha. Fletch could sense her discomfort and was sorry she was in the room with this man he felt might be unstable.

"Mr. Taylor, is it true this is the first acting job you have had in a couple of years?"

"Yes, Detective, I've taken a much-needed break from the acting profession. I only accepted this job because I know my many fans have missed seeing me on screen. I was not sorry when Reggie called it off. I have other things to fill my time."

Pete excused the man, but not before Brad turned to Samantha and said he looked forward to seeing her again very soon.

"I'm sorry, Samantha, I can see Brad Taylor is fixated on you. I would never have had you stay in the room if I'd known. Fletch, keep an eye on Samantha while you're here. Brad Taylor was in trouble for stalking a young woman not too long ago."

"I won't let her out of my sight," Fletch said.

"I'm sure you're safe from Brad Taylor, Samantha. I feel good about Fletch watching over you. Brad's a strange guy but I'm sure he's harmless. He's an aging actor and he's just trying to prove he's still attractive to women."

CHAPTER 11

"I think it's time we call it a day," said Pete. "I wouldn't mind a drink, myself. Anyone up for dinner? There's a steakhouse not too far from here; I haven't been there recently, but it was always good."

"I'm waiting for my mother," said Gina. "She heard about Father on the news and is on her way. I wanted to call her myself, but the reporters beat me to it. I can wait outside for her."

"Don't be silly; we'll wait with you. If she's up to it, she can go with us."

Within the next few minutes, Alexandra Crenshaw pulled into the long driveway. She hugged her daughter and offered condolences. Gina introduced her to everyone.

"I'm sorry for your loss, Mrs. Crenshaw," said Pete. He was amazed at the resemblance Gina had to her mother.

Pete Bellamy had married his high school sweetheart. They had been married for fifteen years when Paula had told him she couldn't take the constant worry of being married to a police officer any longer. Pete was devastated and poured himself into his job even more. He remained close to his children, although he only saw them on the weekends. He hadn't dated in the twelve years since the divorce. Paula had married again, this time to an insurance salesman. He liked her new husband and was glad she'd found happiness with someone who didn't live on the edge of danger.

"Thank you for your kind words, Detective. I'm sorry Reggie's dead, but I haven't had much of a relationship with him for years. I'm here to console my daughter."

Samantha could see the sparks fly between Pete Bellamy and Alexandra Crenshaw, and asked Mrs. Crenshaw if she'd like to join them for dinner.

"Yes, Mom, please join us," said Gina with a twinkle in her eye.

"If I'm not intruding, that would be very nice. Please call me Alexandra."

Pete Bellamy took Alexandra's arm and they walked together to her car.

Samantha, Megan and Gina all grinned their approval as Fletch and Mike wondered what the women were up to.

At the restaurant, the group was seated beside a crackling fire in the dining room. Pete Bellamy stepped out of his role as a homicide detective and felt more relaxed than he had in a very long time. He felt an attraction to Alexandra Crenshaw; she had a softness that was the total opposite of Rachel Ross. He understood why Reggie had been reluctant to divorce her and marry Rachel. If Alexandra was *his* wife, he would never let her go. He'd loved Paula when they were together, but he never considered giving up his career in favor of her. Pete could imagine himself ending his career in law enforcement for a woman like Alexandra.

Gina had never seen her mother with a man before. She often asked Alexandra why she' stayed married to her father. "Gina, dear, if I ever find someone I want to be with, my marriage to your father will be formally ended. Until then, I don't see any reason to do so, he's free to begin proceedings if he chooses."

Because of Father's death, there was no reason now to go through a divorce. *Mom is free to do as she pleases*, Gina thought to herself and then felt ashamed. She didn't mean to be unkind to her father's memory, but she wondered if he deserved her loyalty after abandoning her and her mother years ago.

The pleasant conversation eventually went back to the murder from earlier in the day.

"You all must think I'm cold-hearted," said Alexandra, looking sheepishly around the table. "I am saddened by Reggie's death, but I can't pretend I have feelings for him. I don't care that he walked out on *me*, but he walked out on our daughter too."

"Alexandra," said Pete, "no one is judging you, I assure you." He looked around the table and everyone nodded in agreement. "I shouldn't say this, but I appreciate your honesty even more after witnessing the bogus Mrs. Crenshaw's performance."

"Gina," said Samantha, "why do you think Reggie transferred his holdings to you? Do you think he suspected his life was in danger?"

"Father confided in me that he knew Rachel wasn't planning a long-term relationship with him. He didn't love her either, but because of her beauty, she was an asset to him. My father was a shallow man; I loved him, but I didn't like him very much. I told him when he said he was putting everything he owned in my name that I wasn't comfortable being responsible for that much money. He didn't care; he did it anyway. I've never spent a dime of his money and I don't plan to. Money never made Father happy and now that he's gone, I can begin to give it away to worthwhile causes. Working in a hospital, I know there are many folks who need money to help them with the astronomical cost of medical care."

Samantha thought of Barry Kline; she didn't know how he would feel about accepting Reggie Crenshaw's money, but she would mention his situation to Gina when she had the chance.

Alexandra still worked as a school secretary. She loved working with the children and they all loved her. She was entertaining her new friends with funny stories of the children now. They laughed and were thoroughly enjoying themselves when a familiar voice interrupted their laughter.

"Well, isn't this a happy group? Are you celebrating your father's death, missy? You have all his money now, but you won't have it for long. I'll see to that."

"Rachel, don't make a spectacle of yourself. No one is celebrating anyone's death; we're simply enjoying a meal with friends. I suggest you do the same," said Fletch.

"Fletch, how can you speak to me that way? Come sit with me in the bar. I'll get rid of Melvin; he's drunk anyway and he won't miss me."

"Just leave, Rachel," said a frustrated Fletch.

"You'll be sorry when you remember what it was like with me. You'll make love to little Samantha tonight, but you'll imagine me in your bed." Rachel turned on her heel and walked toward the bar.

"Don't say it," Fletch said to everyone. "I don't know what I saw in her either."

"Fletch, if you want to leave, we'll understand," said Pete Bellamy.

"Don't be silly, I can ignore the woman if you can," Fletch spoke directly to Samantha.

"She doesn't bother me, Fletch," Samantha answered. "I feel sorry for her; it's obvious she's an unhappy person and I would be too if I didn't have you. How about some cheesecake everyone? I saw the waitress serving it at the next table and it looked wonderful."

After the dessert was served and everyone cleaned their plates, Megan looked at her watch. "Samantha, do you suppose we should get our men to the hotel. They're still adjusting to the change in time zones and are probably ready to call it a night."

"It has been a trying day for all of you," said Pete. "Alexandra, would you like me to drive you and Gina home? I'll be happy to pick you up in the morning to retrieve your cars."

Before Alexandra had a chance to answer, Gina spoke up: "Detective, why don't you drive my mother home? I have my car here and I'd feel better if she didn't have to drive that winding road to pick up her car. I didn't notice any street lights out that way."

Alexandra was mortified that her daughter would be so obvious. She lived twenty minutes away and there was no reason Pete Bellamy should drive out of his way to take her home.

"That's a great idea, Gina," Pete smiled. "Blake Lambert will be meeting me at the Seabrook house first thing in the morning. I'm sure he'll want to speak to the representative of your father's affairs regarding the death that took place in his home. That way your mother can tour the estate; it's an interesting place."

They all left the restaurant together without seeing Rachel sitting at a corner table of the bar watching them with venom in her eyes.

*****

"Samantha, this place is amazing," said Fletch, reaching for his wallet. "Who's footing the bill now that Mr. Gottrocks is gone?"

"It's paid for through the week. We were going to move when you guys arrived. There are a few nice hotels in the area that are not quite so lavish."

"Hey, even us lowly cops like lavish occasionally, especially when the price is right. At the moment, I'm only interested in being with my beautiful wife. Where's the bedroom?" he asked with a smile.

After a quick good night, both couples climbed the stairs and walked to the opposite ends of the suite closing the bedroom doors behind them.

"I hope you aren't taking the things Rachel has said to heart, Sam. Seeing her now, I can't remember why I was attracted to her in the first place."

"She's an extremely beautiful woman; any man would be enticed by her."

"You do believe that I'm over her and have been for a very long time. I know she's trying to make you doubt my love for you, but that's not going to happen."

"Joseph Fletcher, don't you have more faith in me than that? I know you love me; you show it every day. I have Rachel to thank for turning you sour on women for so long. If she hadn't broken your heart, you might have been married with two kids when we met and we couldn't do this." Samantha threw her arms around him and pulled him down on the bed. Rachel was far from Fletch's mind for the rest of the night.

*****

"I'm sorry you had to drive all the way out to Santa Monica, Pete. My daughter was being silly. I'm sure I wouldn't have had any trouble driving on a winding road."

"I'm glad to drive you home. I'd like to get to know you better. I find myself attracted to you and that doesn't happen often with this old cop."

"I feel the same way, Pete. I haven't been interested in anyone since Reggie and I were first married. I was young and stupid and fell for his charm. I know I should have divorced the man years ago, but this way I could always say I'm a married woman. It was an excuse, I'm afraid."

"My wife told me she didn't want to be married to a cop. That was after we had two kids. We were high school sweethearts and maybe we married because that was what was expected of us. She's happy with someone else now in a safe line of work, and I'm alone with no one to worry about me."

"What about your children? Do you see them?"

"Yes, they're both grown now, but they do take pity on their old man and spend time with me as often as they can. Gina is a special young woman; I know you must be proud of her."

"Gina is wonderful. Reggie loved his daughter although he found it difficult to show affection. I know Gina loved her father too. She understood his flaws and looked beyond them. I think his happiest times were when the two of them were together. I'm afraid Reggie's last years with Rachel were the least happy of his life."

Pete drove into the driveway of a modest home on a tree-lined street. He expected a billionaire's wife would be living in a mansion with a butler opening the door for the mistress of the household.

"You thought I'd be living in a fancy place in an upscale neighborhood, didn't you?"

"No, I thought you'd be living in a mansion dripping with servants. I'm glad I was wrong. I like this house; it suits you."

"Reggie hated it; he never forgave me for moving out of the house we shared. It wasn't a mansion, but it was too big for Gina and me. I couldn't keep it up myself and couldn't afford gardeners and maid service on my salary."

"You didn't want his money, I take it. Gina is a lot like her mother; she's lucky she had you to influence her choices."

Pete walked her to the door. "I'd ask you in, but it's getting late and you have a busy day tomorrow. Gina will be picking me up at the crack of dawn and I need my beauty sleep too."

Pete took her hand and then found that he couldn't resist kissing her lips gently. "I'd like to see you again, Alexandra."

Alexandra was pleasantly surprised at how much she enjoyed Pete's kiss. "I'd like that, Pete. I'll see you in the morning when Gina drops me off to pick up my car."

"I'll look forward to it," he said and walked back to his car. Detective Peter Bellamy had a difficult time keeping the smile off his face all the way home.

Alexandra Crenshaw spun around when she closed her front door. She felt like a teenager again and danced all the way up the stairs. She'd have to remember to thank Gina for a perfectly lovely evening.

# CHAPTER 12

Blake Lambert slept better than he thought he would on the airplane. Just before landing, he called the property manager who oversaw the rental of the Seabrook house for the movie.

"Tell me more about what happened yesterday," he said.

"I'm sorry, Mr. Lambert. I can't give you much information; the police suspect it was foul play, but they aren't giving any specifics."

Blake Lambert was usually a patient man, but this whole situation was getting the better of him. The mansion had been an albatross around his neck. He'd bought the place because he loved his grandmother and she loved telling stories of the activities in the old mansion. He realized when he grew older that the stories had never happened and they were all in Jasmine's mind.

He'd spent a small fortune on repairs and now someone had died in the pool the previous owners had built. He didn't know why he'd agreed to allow the movie company to film on location in and outside the house. Myra Sims was a friend of his secretary, Susan, in his Los Angeles office. Myra was trying to make a name for herself in the movie industry. She was a professional real estate home stager and wanted to branch out to set decoration. She'd read about the movie in a trade magazine and knew the history of the Seabrook Shores estate and that it belonged to Susan's boss.

"Myra, I can't ask Mr. Lambert to recommend you for this job. He has nothing to do with the movie."

Myra ignored her friend and took it upon herself to contact Blake personally. She used her friendship with Susan to persuade him to recommend her for the job. She convinced him that the house would sell at a higher price if it was furnished in period pieces. He was anxious to get the movie over with and get the house sold and agreed to recommend her.

He told Susan of her friend's request and she was appalled that Myra had gone behind her back and used her name to influence Mr. Lambert.

"I'm so sorry, Mr. Lambert, I had no idea Myra would do such a thing."

"Don't concern yourself, Susan. If it helps to sell the place, I'll be forever grateful."

Now, the movie wouldn't be made and Myra was out of a job. *As soon as this investigation is over, I'll sell it at a loss. I'm sure I can't get what I put into it because of the possibility of murder in the place, but I don't care any more,* Blake thought to himself.

*****

Pete Bellamy arrived at the mansion before seven o'clock. His meeting with Blake Lambert wouldn't take place for another hour or more, but he wanted to make sure he didn't miss seeing Alexandra when Gina brought her to retrieve her car.

"Mom," said Gina, "I hope we aren't too early to run into Detective Bellamy. I have a meeting scheduled this morning and I can't get out of it."

"What makes you think I'd be interested in seeing the detective again?" asked Alexandra, trying to hide her grin.

"Mom, you've never been able to hide your feelings; it's obvious sparks were flying between you and the cop. Don't get me wrong; I think it's wonderful. It's time you had a man in your life."

"I've done very well without a man for many years. I think you and I had a pretty good life so far."

"It is a good life, but now that I'm out of our house and living on my own, don't you think it would be nice to spend some time with a male friend?"

"I shouldn't mention this because you won't let me forget it, Gina, but Pete kissed me goodnight when he dropped me off. It's been years since a man kissed me on the lips. I have to admit, I liked it."

"Mom, that's wonderful. I knew you two were hitting it off. Samantha and Megan felt it too. I'm happy for you. Isn't it ironic that because of Father, Detective Bellamy is in your life. I'm glad Father did one thing good for you."

"Gina, your father gave me the best thing I could ask for when you were born. Oh, look, Pete's car is here; I can feel a flutter in my heart. I'm acting like a teenager."

Gina laughed at her mother; she *was* acting like a teenager and it looked good on her. Watching the detective smile as he walked to the car, she could tell Pete Bellamy was feeling like a kid himself.

"It's good to see you both again," Pete said, while looking into Alexandra's eyes. "I was hoping to see you before you left for school."

"School is out for the week, Detective. My mother is free today. Unfortunately, I have a meeting this morning that I can't get out of and must leave. I shouldn't be more than a couple of hours; I hope I don't miss Mr. Lambert, I'd like to pay him for the use of the house and apologize for what happened here yesterday."

"I talked to him this morning; he sounds like a reasonable guy. I get the feeling he wants to be done with this mess and get moving on the sale of the house. I'll ask him to wait for you if he has the time."

"I'd like to talk to him and ask why he bought this old place. It's obvious it hasn't been lived in for a long time. It's a beautiful, stately manor and should be appreciated.

It's not my preference, but I'm sure there are some people who would love to live in a place like this."

"Gina, it's none of your business. I don't think you should question Mr. Lambert's motives in buying this place," said her mother.

"You're right, Mom. I won't badger the poor guy. You two have fun this morning and I'll see you in a couple of hours. You'll still be here, right, Mom?"

"If I'm not in the way, I'd like to wait until the others get here. I had such a nice time with everyone last night."

"You won't be in the way at all and you can keep me company," said Detective Bellamy.

Gina smiled as she drove away; she knew she'd left her mother in good hands. *Now, if I could only find some-one who makes me feel like a teenager again,* she sighed.

*****

Megan had her hand outstretched on the table when Samantha and Fletch met Mike and her in the coffee shop.

"Hey, Ms. Always Observant, are you not seeing something new?"

"Megan, your ring! You're engaged! I can't believe I didn't notice."

The friends hugged and the men shook hands. The entire conversation through breakfast was wedding talk. Samantha wanted to know every word the two of them spoke. Mike told them Megan proposed before he could say the words. Megan said she was afraid he'd given up asking her and had decided not to take any chances. Mike was ready with the ring he'd carried in his pocket for months. They hadn't set a date, but didn't want to wait too long.

"I want to go from here to Las Vegas, but she thinks her mother will never forgive her if she elopes. My mother wouldn't be happy about that either. I better resign myself to waiting, but it will be worth it," Mike said.

"I'm calling Mom and Dad after breakfast. I'll tell them we want a simple ceremony and a small reception. My mother is a lot like yours; she'll do what she wants. Yours was a lovely wedding even though it was filled with intrigue throughout."

Megan and Mike planned to spend the day at the pool and relax in the California sunshine while Samantha and Fletch returned to Seabrook Shores.

*****

"It's wonderful news about Megan and Mike," said Samantha while Fletch entered the freeway on their way to Seabrook Shores. "I thought she was softening to the idea of marriage. Jimmy is a distant memory for her and she's able to move on now. Mike is so unlike Jimmy; I can't imagine Megan ever falling for that sleaze."

"You're probably wondering what I saw in Rachel," Fletch said in a low voice.

"Fletch, Rachel is a beautiful woman; it's not surprising that you were attracted to her. I can't say I like knowing you loved another, but I do understand. I saw the charming side of her when she was flirting with Grant Wagner. That poor guy was mesmerized by her attention. If Reggie hadn't forced her to leave the party that night, I'm afraid Rachel would have had him and ruined things with the girl he loves."

"He seems like a nice kid; I think he saw a different side of her yesterday. She wasn't like that when I knew her, at least I didn't think so."

Samantha patted his arm. She was secure in their love for each other, and Rachel Ross was no threat to her.

"Fletch, something has nagged at me about the study in the mansion. Something was different in the room; I'm anxious to have a look again, maybe it will trigger a memory."

*****

"Alexandra, I'm happy to see you again," said Pete Bellamy. "I had a wonderful time last night. Maybe it's inappropriate to be enjoying your company while investigating your husband's murder."

"I have been Reggie's wife in name only for over twenty years. I'm sorry he's dead, but I can't mourn him. He was a stranger to me for many of those years. He only had time for Gina at his convenience. I don't think he knew how to be a father; I doubt he ever acknowledged Gina's existence except to his lawyer all these years. I'm ashamed I married such a self-centered man."

"Wasn't there anyone in your life after you and Reggie parted ways?"

"No, my concern was only for Gina. I tried to make up for her lack of a real father and that didn't allow for other men in my life."

"Do you think you might be able to allow a man in your life now?"

"I already have," Alexandra smiled when she took Pete's arm as they walked into the mansion.

*****

*They're back again*, he thought to himself. *I'm glad I stayed up late last night to get everything ready. It was a long walk from the marina parking lot, but it was worth it because they'll never look for my car there.*

He'd hung the dress on a satin hanger in the bedroom, standing back to admire his choice. He didn't think Pearl had seen him when he'd slipped into the costume storage room at the studio. Everyone knew him there and didn't think it unusual to see him wandering around near the storeroom. He wouldn't make the same mistake he did with Tiffany. This time, he'd make sure he had the girl all to himself. She'd forget about that guy and they would be happy together.

Brad looked out the peephole in the wall. He watched as that detective walked into the study with a woman he hadn't seen before. He looked away when he saw Pete take Alexandra in arms and kiss her. The sight upset him; it reminded him of seeing Mama in the clutches of that horrible man.

## CHAPTER 13

"Detective Bellamy is here," said Samantha, "I'll bet he came early hoping to see Alexandra before Gina dropped her off to pick up her car."

"You and your buddy, Megan, should go into the matchmaking business; you won't be happy until everyone in the world is hitched," teased Fletch.

Samantha ignored him and walked to the front door just as it opened. Pete and Alexandra stood side by side in the foyer each with sheepish grins on their faces.

"Hello, you two; it looks like you're enjoying your morning so far," said Samantha.

Alexandra felt embarrassed and wondered if her lipstick was smeared. She stammered nervously when she said: "Gina dropped me off to get my car; she had a meeting this morning and couldn't stay. Pete offered to show me around the place; I hope I'm not in the way."

Samantha smiled and told them she was happy to see them both. Fletch shook Pete's hand. He would never admit it to Samantha, but he was glad these two had found each other.

"Detective Bellamy," Samantha said, using his official title, "I'd like to have another look at the study if you don't mind. I have a feeling I'm missing something and I hope seeing the room will jog my memory."

"I need all the help I can get in this case. I haven't ruled out any of the folks who were here yesterday, except for you and Megan."

"Megan wouldn't have any reason to want Mr. Crenshaw dead, but I did have an interest in having this movie made. I don't think you should rule anyone out, including me," said Samantha in all seriousness.

"You might have a motive if the movie was true to your book, but I suspect you were relieved when Reggie called the whole thing off."

"You're right, Detective. I'm not sorry about that at all."

\*\*\*\*\*

Samantha and the others walked into the study. Samantha looked around the room surveying every object on the desk and credenza. Something was missing from the credenza. She tried to picture what it looked like when she first saw the room with Myra Sims.

"I thought seeing the room would help, but I'm drawing a blank."

"Sam will ponder this until she remembers. I trust her instincts; she's a pretty good detective," Fletch said with pride.

\*\*\*\*\*

Blake Lambert pulled into the winding driveway. He could feel the resentment building as he came closer to the mansion. *Grandmother Jasmine, why did I feel drawn to this place? It's almost like you wanted me to find it for a reason. Although I can't imagine what that reason is. It has caused me nothing but headaches since I bought it and now some poor guy has been murdered on the premises,* he thought.

Samantha expected Mr. Lambert to be an older English gentleman and was surprised to see a handsome young man with only a slight British accent enter the house. His sandy-colored hair was tousled from the drive in a rented convertible. He apologized for his appearance. "I like to brag to my friends that I drove a convertible in February when I go back home," he said with a grin.

Samantha liked this Englishman. He was down to earth, unlike the stereotype she had in mind. He told the

group he'd made a sentimental decision when he'd purchased the house and he'd regretted it ever since. He
agreed to wait for Gina Crenshaw's arrival, but didn't
feel she owed him an apology.

"It's unfortunate that a death took place here, but I
don't blame Mr. Crenshaw; I'm sure he would have preferred not being the victim of the crime himself."

Gina's meeting lasted longer than she'd anticipated
and she hoped she hadn't missed Mr. Lambert. She pulled
her car into the driveway and was happy to see her mother's car hadn't been moved. Gina knew her mother was
capable of having a full life without a man in it, but was
hoping the sparks were still flying between her mom and
Pete Bellamy. She noticed a sporty convertible with the
top down. Could that be Mr. Lambert's car? *The old guy
must be going through his second childhood driving that*,
she thought and smiled.

Gina walked into the mansion and was greeted by her
mother and Detective Bellamy. She was happy to see
Samantha and Fletch in the parlor also. She wondered
where the old English gentleman was and spotted a handsome, young man with beautiful blue eyes. He held out
his hand and introduced himself.

Gina felt herself blushing when she said: "Mr. Lambert, I didn't expect you to be so young. I'm sorry, I
didn't mean to blurt that out. I'm happy to meet you."

"I know we English have a reputation with you Yan-
kees of being a tad formal, but I wish you'd call me
Blake."

Samantha could see a light shining in Gina's eyes
matched by the look on Blake Lambert's face. Fletch
watched his wife and knew she would make sure the first
meeting of these young people would not be their last.

Fletch and Detective Bellamy found a quiet corner
where they discussed the possible suspects in the case.
Alexandra excused herself with the promise of returning

in the early afternoon to meet Pete for lunch. Blake and Gina walked toward the ocean, anxious to get to know each other better. Samantha wandered into the study again, trying to jog her memory.

She was startled when she heard a deep voice say: "Are you looking for this Samantha?"

She turned and saw Brad Taylor standing by the bookcases, holding an ornate, antique clock.

"Brad, I didn't hear you come in," she said with a slight tremor in her voice. "That's it; that's what was missing on the credenza. Where did you find it?" She walked to him and he grabbed her arm, pulling her into a small opening in the bookcase. She heard the door close behind her and fought the feeling of sheer panic.

"What is this place?" she heard herself saying. Her eyes were adjusting to the darkness after being in the study with the bright sunshine beaming through the windows. She saw a fire in a fireplace and candles glowing. A dress hung from the doorway, it was blue and white with puffy sleeves and a billowing skirt with a crinoline petticoat under it. Little Bo Peep came to mind as she glanced in disbelief at the dress.

"Brad, I don't know what this is all about, but I can't stay in here with you. Where's the door?"

"My darling, Samantha, you don't want to leave, you and I are meant to be together. Now, go into the bedroom and put on this lovely dress I picked out just for you."

"Brad, I'm not going to put on that stupid dress, let me out of here now. My husband and Detective Bellamy are in the other room. If I scream, they'll hear me and you'll be in big trouble. Let me out now and I won't tell anyone you're here."

"No one will hear you; this is a secret hide-a-way and it's soundproof. Forget about that guy, you and I will be together forever. Now, be a good little princess and put on the dress." His voice was becoming harsher and Samantha's fear was growing. She'd put on the dress if it meant she could buy some time. Surely Fletch would miss her and wonder where she was. How did Brad get her into this room? She didn't see a door by the bookcases. In the movies, there was always a button someone pushed to enter a secret room. Could it be this old place had something like that? Samantha was terrified but determined to stay calm. The bedroom was cordoned off by a heavy curtain. She pulled it as tight as she could and slipped into the dress. It smelled like mothballs and the petticoat scratched her legs as she walked out into the room, feeling ridiculous in the Bo Peep dress.

"Oh, my dear, you look so lovely, but your hair and makeup will never do." Brad took her hand and walked to the far end of the room where he sat her down at a dressing table. He flipped a switch and bright lights shone all around the mirror. *This looks like the dressing room of a movie studio,* she thought. *This guy is crazy.*

Brad picked up a curling iron and began curling her hair until she had ringlets covering her head. He then took a cleansing wipe and removed all her makeup. She was thankful she hadn't put too much on this morning although he was being gentle.

"Brad, may I ask why you're doing this? I'm beginning to look like a porcelain doll."

He ignored her and brought out a box filled with makeup; he began with her cheeks and painted bright red circles on both. He put thick bright blue eye shadow on her eyelids and drew exaggerated eyelashes above and below her eyes. He then put ruby-red lipstick on her lips, making them look bow-like. When he was finished with the makeup, he put bows in her hair and stood back admiring his work. He held her hand and led her to the sofa, placing her in the center. He sat across from her and stared at her until she began to cry out of the frustration of not knowing how to get out of this mess.

"Don't do that!" he shouted. He grabbed her arm and took her back to the dressing table. He picked up the cleansing cloth, removing the makeup and began again, starting with her cheeks. Samantha's face felt chafed and sore because of the heavy makeup. She knew she had to control her tears or he'd continue to make her up until her skin was raw. *Where are you Fletch? I need you!* she thought.

*****

"Sir, the suspects have all agreed to come to the station in an hour for further questioning—all except one. We haven't been able to find Brad Taylor. His housekeeper said his bed hasn't been slept in and she doesn't think he came home last night."

"That's not unusual for a movie star. Maybe he found a diversion and spent the night with her."

"Maybe, but the housekeeper said she was worried. She told me Mr. Taylor is always home at night. She said he never goes out after dinner and he wasn't home for dinner either. She thinks he might be in trouble. I got the feeling she has reason to worry, but she didn't want to say too much."

"Thanks, Hendricks. Keep on it. Maybe I'll visit the housekeeper myself. If she's hiding something, we need to know."

While Pete was on the phone, Fletch looked for Samantha; he was walking through each room on the first floor when Pete stopped him.

"Fletch, you look worried; what's going on?"

"I can't find Samantha and I have a feeling in my gut that she's in trouble. I'm going to check upstairs. She seems to have disappeared." Fletch ran up to the second-floor, calling her name. After checking the third floor, he came back down and out to the grounds. Gina and Blake were walking back toward the house.

"Did Samantha come out this way?"

"No, Fletch, we haven't seen her since we left the house. Have you checked the other floors?"

"I've covered every inch of the place; Pete even looked in the basement. He had a call from the station, and Brad Taylor's whereabouts is unknown. He took an unusual interest in Samantha the other day. Have you seen him around here today?"

"No one has been here except us, Fletch. What can we do to help find her? Do you think she left the property?"

"I know she wouldn't do that without telling me. Where would she go? The next house is a quarter mile up the road and I don't know what reason she would have to go there."

"Blake," said Gina, "you look deep in thought; do you know something that could help Fletch?"

"I can't be sure, but I recall my grandmother talking about a secret room. I believed her when I was a kid, but she told so many stories about this old place, I hadn't thought about that possibility for years. I have a copy of the blueprints at the office. I'll have my assistant message me a copy." Brad called his office. Susan could sense the urgency in his voice and did as he asked. Blake told the group the blueprints were on the way.

Pete was on the phone demanding to be sent any information his officers could find about Brad Taylor. "I don't care how insignificant it seems, I want everything!"

*****

Megan called Samantha's cell phone and was concerned when she wasn't able to reach her. She placed a call to Fletch to see if everything was okay.

"Samantha is missing, Megan. I don't know where her phone is; I tried calling her myself and it went right to voicemail."

"Mike and I will rent a car and be there as soon as we can. Maybe she'll turn up before then."

*****

Pete's phone rang and the information he'd asked for started pouring in. He looked worried when he was finished reading everything his men had found about Brad Taylor.

"Brad Taylor's real name is Sonny Lee; he has a twin sister named Sally. Their mother, who suffers from dementia, is in a home in Fairfield. Before she retired, she worked as a makeup artist at Willington Studios. According to the staff at the home, she talks about her twins as though they're toddlers. The old timers at the studio remember her painting the kids' faces with pink circle cheeks and exaggerated eyelashes and prancing them in front of the movie people. Neither one of the kids could dance or sing, but that didn't stop her from continuing to try to audition them until they were almost teenagers.

"Sally Lee ran off with some kid when she was only fifteen. She never returned to Los Angeles and is living in a small town in Wisconsin. She's married and has a couple of grown children. My officer has contacted the sheriff's office in the town and he's waiting for the sheriff's report.

"Not much is known about Sonny from the time his sister left until he changed his name to Brad Taylor and was lucky enough to make it as an actor. He has never married and has only been photographed with women in publicity shots. He hasn't had a starring role in several years and came out of semi-retirement to do Samantha's film."

CHAPTER 14

In a small town in northeast Wisconsin, Sally Rafferty
wiped down the last table in the truck stop off the main
highway. She greeted the sheriff by name when he entered the restaurant.

"Hi, Harvey, what brings you out this way? You're
late for breakfast and early for lunch."

"Hello, Sally, I'm not here for food. I hoped you could
help me with information that will help with an investigation of a missing person in Los Angeles."

"Who's missing, Harvey? I don't know what help I
can be."

"Sally, do you know of a fellow named Brad Taylor or
maybe you know him by his given name, Sonny Lee?"

Sally lowered her eyes; she pointed to a table away
from the counter and asked the sheriff if they could sit
there. She regained her composure and spoke: "Sonny
Lee is my twin brother. Is Sonny in trouble, Harvey?"
She looked as if she feared the answer.

"I don't know the details, Sally; the Los Angeles Police Department is investigating and asked that I question
you. You don't have to tell me what, if anything, you
know about your brother. From the information I do have,
he might be involved in the disappearance of a young
woman in California."

"I'll tell you anything I can, Harvey, but I'm afraid I
don't know much about Sonny anymore.

"I left home when I was barely fifteen. I ran off with a
boy in my class. We played house for a while until his
money ran out and he took a bus back home. I couldn't
face going back to the apartment I'd lived in with Sonny

and my mother. I ended up on the streets and was picked up by the police. When they discovered my age, I was turned over to social services and placed in a foster home in town here. I don't know if you remember the Bakers on Mulberry Court; they've passed on now, but they took me in and treated me as one of their own. They had three grown children by then and all welcomed me into the family.

"They saw to it that I finished high school. I had a job in this diner after school and during the summer. This is where Will and I met over thirty years ago. This place has been in Will's family since it opened and together we have managed it for all these years.

"You don't want to hear about me; you asked about Sonny. I was just a kid, but I knew something was very wrong with my mother. I never knew who my dad was; Mama never mentioned him and I was afraid to ask. Mama had a temper and if we ever said anything she didn't like; she'd swat us and swat us hard.

"Mama worked at a movie studio; she was a makeup artist and could work magic on the faces of some of the actresses who weren't as perfect in real-life as they were on screen.

"Mama set up a dressing room in the corner of our living room. I can't remember a time when she didn't make Sonny and me up and dress us in costumes she'd borrowed from the studio. I don't remember when this nightly ritual began to be a chore, but I dreaded going home after school because I knew she would be making us up and then scrubbing our faces clean before we went to bed. Sonny never complained; he said he loved Mama and she was happiest when she was painting our faces.

"I'm not sure when it was that Mama met Uncle George. He wasn't our uncle, but Mama insisted we call him that. He wasn't mean to us, but it was obvious he would have preferred to be alone with Mama without kids underfoot. Mama got rid of all the makeup and threw the dressing table in the dumpster in the alley after George started to come by in the evenings.

"Sonny and I were young, but old enough to know what was going on in the next room. I covered my ears and could ignore them, but Sonny couldn't sleep until he heard George snoring.

"One day we came home from school and Mama was on the sofa crying. There was a half-bottle of whiskey on the coffee table. Somehow we knew we'd seen the last of Uncle George.

"After that day, Mama became more and more dependent on Sonny. She continued to work at her job, but when she was home she would cling to Sonny and pat his head. Sonny seemed to enjoy it and the two were in their own little world. Sonny never had any friends in school. Mama told us she didn't want anyone in our apartment. I had more friends than Sonny, but only during school hours. Corey Singer was in my English class. He asked me to the sophomore dance and knowing Mama wouldn't allow it, I told her I was sick and was going to bed. I put pillows under the covers and climbed out the window to meet Corey.

"I hadn't fooled Mama and was forced to face her wrath when I returned home at nine o'clock that night. She threatened to keep me out of school for the next three years. When she went off to work the next day, I called Corey to tell him Mama had caught me and I wouldn't be going to school anymore. He came over to the apartment and complained that his dad was giving him a hard time about his studies. That was when we decided to run off together. Corey had saved money for college from his paper route and mowing lawns. He had a little over five hundred dollars and we were sure that would be enough money to last us until we were sixteen and able to get jobs. As you can imagine, that money was gone before the month was out. Corey decided starvation was not for him, called his folks and was on the next bus back to Los Angeles. He begged me to come with him, but I couldn't face going back to that life. I doubt Mama and Sonny missed having me around; I was the third wheel in the relationship. I'm not implying there was anything inappropriate going on between Mama and Sonny, but their devotion to each other was peculiar, to say the least."

"Sally, I'm sorry to hear of your hardships early in life," said the sheriff. "Tell me, do you look anything like your mother?"

"There is a resemblance; I have a picture of her in my .office. It was taken when she was in her early thirties, I don't care to ever see her again, but something has made me keep that photo all these years."

She excused herself to retrieve the photo and handed it to the sheriff.

Sally was right about a resemblance; the photo was of a woman younger than Sally, but quite beautiful. "Do you mind if I take this to have it copied and sent to the folks in Los Angeles. It might be of help to them in their investigation. I'll handle it with care and get it back to you as soon as possible."

"Do whatever you have to do Harvey. If someone is in danger because of Sonny, I want to help in any way I can."

## CHAPTER 15

A calm came over Samantha; she knew in her heart Brad wouldn't hurt her. He was living in a fantasy world and she was simply a prop. She thought if she could get him to open up to her, he might come out of the trance he seemed to be in.

"Brad, when did you decide to act in movies? The first time I saw you was when you co-starred with Anna Carlson in *Midnight Skies*. My brother, Dennis, took me to see that movie. He's a big fan of yours."

"I remember that movie. I liked kissing Anna; she's very pretty and she smelled good." Brad smiled as if remembering a happy time in his life and suddenly his expression changed to sadness. "Mama didn't like Anna. She told her to leave me alone and Anna didn't talk to me anymore after that."

"Did your mama like any of your friends, Brad?"

"Oh, I never had friends. When Sally left, it was just Mama and me. Mama said she loved me best anyway. It makes me sad that Mama is in that awful place. She doesn't know my name anymore. Her hair used to be so beautiful and now it's all stringy and ugly."

He sat next to Samantha and gently touched her hair. "Mama's hair was this color too. She let me brush it for her. Would you like me to brush your hair for you?"

"If you'd like to brush my hair, that would be nice, Brad."

"I can't brush your hair, silly, the curls will come out." He laughed like a child. "Maybe I can just touch it."

"Is Sally your sister, Brad?"

"She was my sister but she ran away. Mama said she sleeps in gutters at night and doesn't have anybody to love her. Mama says I'm lucky because I have her and we will be together forever. You aren't Mama, are you, Samantha?"

"No, Brad, I'm not your mama, but I'd like to be your friend. Tell me, did you hurt Mr. Crenshaw?"

"Mr. Crenshaw is a mean man. I don't like him." Brad sat across from her again, staring at Samantha and not saying another word.

*****

Blake's assistant sent him copies of the original blueprints of the house. After carefully examining them, they discovered there was indeed a secret room behind the bookcases in the study.

Fletch was ready to tear the bookcase apart to find a way in to rescue Samantha. Pete pulled him back. "We don't know what Brad Taylor is capable of, Fletch. Samantha could be in danger if we aren't cautious."

Inside the room, Brad walked over to the peephole, "They're here for you, Samantha. They think I'm going to hurt you, but you're my friend, aren't you?"

"Yes, Brad, I'm your friend. It's time to leave this room."

"All right, Samantha." He smiled and pushed a button. The bookcase opened and Brad stepped into the study with Samantha following.

Fletch was shocked to see his wife covered in curls with ridiculous makeup on her face and wearing a frilly dress. He was torn between hugging her and slugging Brad.

"Samantha, are you okay? What did that maniac do to you?"

"I'm fine, Fletch. Brad didn't hurt me. He made me look like a movie star."

"Samantha isn't a movie star,; she's my friend," he said proudly.

"Don't let them hurt him, Detective Bellamy. Brad didn't mean any harm."

After the officers walked Brad out of the mansion and into a waiting transport car, Samantha told Pete about the clock that was missing on the credenza and that it was in that room. She asked if she could change out of the dress and into her own clothes. She couldn't wait to brush the curls out of her hair and wash the makeup off her face. Gina offered to help her to get out of the billowing dress.

Pete picked up the ornate clock, placing it in a plastic bag. "We'll have this tested for traces of blood. I'll bet the lab will verify Crenshaw's blood is a match and we will have our culprit. Samantha, if you'll come down to the station when you're up to it, you can press charges against Brad Taylor for kidnapping."

"Detective, Brad is a sick man, but I don't believe he's a murderer. He didn't hurt anything but my dignity and I won't be pressing charges."

"Samantha, that's your choice, but we have him in possession of the object that most likely contributed to a man's death. I can't overlook that fact."

Megan arrived and rushed to Samantha's side. "Samantha, what did he do to you? I should have been with you today. I'm so sorry."

"I'm fine, Megan; once I get this clown makeup off and these curls out of my hair, I'll be happy, and I'll be looking for the real culprit in this case. I know it's not Brad Taylor."

"Sam, why are you so sure it's not Brad?" asked Fletch.

"Brad's fantasy world doesn't include murder. His mother did a number on the guy for years. I'm guessing she's in a nursing home now and that she's suffered from mental illness for quite some time."

"I have to get to the station to meet with the others who were here yesterday. I trust your instincts about Brad, Samantha, but I can't help but wonder how he ended up with the clock in his possession," said Detective Bellamy.

"It's possible Brad saw the entire incident yesterday, but I don't know if he can distinguish between reality and fantasy," Samantha said.

*****

Pete Bellamy called Alexandra to make sure she got home all right. "I'm sorry but I won't be able to make lunch today," he said. "I'd like very much to see you again, Alexandra. Would you like to have dinner this evening? I hope to be free shortly after seven o'clock."

"That would be lovely, Pete. I'll be ready when you call." Alexandra had waited long enough for someone to enter her life and didn't care if she acted like a desperate woman; she knew she wanted Pete Bellamy in her life.

*****

"Sam, weren't you the least bit frightened of Brad Taylor today? It was so creepy the way he always looked at you," asked Megan.

"When he first grabbed me, I was terrified. I was sure he was going to kill me or worse. As I sat there with my face itching from the makeup, I began to see him as a frightened little boy. His relationship with his mother was unnatural. It sounds like the woman drove his sister away and then told Brad she was lying in the gutter somewhere. He wasn't allowed to have friends and when he did find himself attracted to a girl, she put the kibosh on the relationship before it even started."

"Leave it to you, Sam, to psychoanalyze your kidnapper," said Fletch. "Your soft heart is one of the many reasons I fell in love with you. I think we should go back to the hotel and relax by the pool after your ordeal."

"Fletch, I want to go to the police station. Maybe we can find out how the interviews are going. One of those people caused injury to Reggie Crenshaw and I'd like to know who."

*****

Alone in the mansion with Gina, Blake talked about the stories his grandmother had told him when he was young.

"I think it's wonderful that you bought this place because of her. She must have been very important in your life, Blake, for you to remember her so fondly all these years."

"She was a character; I know she loved my grandfather, but I don't think she ever got over her feelings for Hawthorne Stonehill. In her mind, was a princess in the castle when she lived here. I'm sure the poor woman was delusional, but I loved hearing her stories just the same."

"Blake, I'm sorry for the trouble my father has caused when he allowed Rachel's movie to be made here. I want to compensate you for the cost of getting this place in shape again."

"Gina, there isn't any damage. I'm going to have that secret room opened though, before anyone else is trapped in there. It's funny, this house has changed hands several times and I don't think anyone knew about the secret room. Brad Taylor is here for only a couple of days and discovered it."

"I can't believe he's the same Brad Taylor who has been in dozens of movies. I can remember watching his films with my mother. She thought he was dreamy. He wasn't my type and a little too old. Who would have guessed he was deranged? I'm not sure my mother recognized him, but she'll be heartbroken."

"What type do you like?"

"Well," Gina said with a smirk, "I'm partial to the studious kind of guy, one who can make me laugh and make me think at the same time. I can do without the macho men of the world."

Blake reached in his jacket pocket and pulled out a pair of horn rimmed glasses, putting them on. "Is this studious enough for you?"

"Yes, and you made me laugh too."

"Here's something to think about; would you like to go out with me tonight?"

"I'd like that very much, Blake."

Blake wanted to take her in his arms but didn't want to scare her away. He didn't know it, but Gina wasn't about to go anywhere.

## CHAPTER 16

When Samantha and the others arrived at the police station, Barry Kline and Grant Wagner were in the waiting room. An attractive woman sat next to Barry with a worried look on her face. Samantha thought it must be his wife, Andie.

Rachel Ross was on the other side of the room. The minute she saw Fletch, she was out of her chair and hanging on his arm.

"Fletch, darling, I knew you'd come to my rescue. That awful detective is going to badger me about poor Reggie, I just know it. I didn't hurt him, I promise."

Fletch pulled her hands away and told her to tell the truth and she wouldn't have to worry. He stood closer to Samantha than he needed to, but he wasn't taking any chances that Rachel would get her claws in him again. He didn't remember her being like this. Her so-called *marriage* to Reggie Crenshaw must have turned her into a clinging vine.

Melvin Kessler wandered into the waiting room after taking a smoke break. "How much longer is this going to take? I'm a busy man and don't have time for this nonsense."

The officer at the desk remained calm and told him to have a seat and someone would be with him shortly.

Detective Bellamy was waiting for the stenographer to finish a different case investigation and would call in his first suspect when she was available. In the meantime, he was observing the group through a two-way mirror. Melvin and Rachel were still being obnoxious and the questioning to come hadn't fazed them in the least. Grant looked like he'd lost his best friend and only smiled briefly when Samantha and Megan greeted him. Unfortunately, Barry Kline's reaction was one of sheer panic as if he'd been caught with his hand in the cookie jar. Pete's gut feeling told him Barry was the person responsible for the injury to Reggie Crenshaw. The poor guy was in debt because of his son's illness; and he was afraid he couldn't keep his family in their home without the money he'd be receiving when the movie was released. Now, there'd be no movie and no money to save his neck. Pete wondered if he'd confided in his wife. She looked as worried as her husband. *Sometimes I loathe this job,* Pete thought to himself, when he heard Carol, the stenographer, knocking on the door.

"Sorry to keep you waiting, Pete. It's been one of those days. It looks like we have a few nervous folks out there."

"Yep, some more than others. I'm going to call Barry Kline first; he's a nice man, but he's acting like he has something to hide."

Pete stepped out of his office. "Sorry to keep you waiting, folks. We're ready for questioning now. Mr. Kline, will you come into my office please."

Barry turned to his wife and mouthed the words *I love you,* squeezing her hand. Samantha watched him walk slowly to the interrogation room and gave him a smile and a thumbs up sign. She walked over to the woman waiting with him and introduced herself. "You must be Barry's wife, Andie?"

"Yes, Samantha; it's so nice to meet you. Barry talked about your book and I picked up a copy for myself. It's a beautiful story about a remarkable man."

"Thank you, Andie. May I call you Andie? Barry talked about you so often in the last few days that I feel like we're old friends."

"I know Barry liked working with you; he didn't like what they did to your story, but he didn't hurt anyone. I'm sure of it, Samantha."

"I'm sure Barry isn't capable of hurting anyone either. Everyone who was at the house yesterday is being questioned. Detective Bellamy is a very fair man. He's jut trying to get answers. I know how you feel; I was a suspect in Professor Stonehill's murder."

"That's right, and you ended up with the detective in that case." Andie looked toward Fletch. "Is that your guy?"

"Yes, that's Detective Joseph Fletch, better known as Fletch."

"Well, he could arrest me anytime; don't tell Barry I said that," she said and giggled.

*****

"Mr. Kline, I'll be asking you a few questions while Ms. Hughes records our meeting. I know we went over your story yesterday, but I'd like to hear it again. Why did you stay in the mansion after Reggie Crenshaw told everyone to leave?"

"I stayed because I wanted to talk to Grant Wagner. He's a talented young man and I believed he would be able to write a screenplay worthy of Samantha Degan's novel. I know people in the major studios and I hooped there might be a chance to sell the concept to one of them. I can assure you, Detective, I never went anywhere near the study or the pool area."

After questioning Barry for the next twenty minutes, Pete was almost certain the man was innocent of any crime. He admitted that he was desperate to earn enough to cover his financial troubles and was disappointed when Reggie reneged on the project.

"Detective," Barry continued, "I admit I was hopping mad about losing money. My family means the world to me and I didn't want to face having to move from the only home the kids have known, but there's no comparison between a house and a man's life."

Pete Bellamy had experienced many con artists in his time; many were masters at covering for themselves. He usually knew when he was being conned. He was convinced Barry Kline was a decent man who was telling the truth. If not, he was a very gifted fraud.

Pete opened the door, thanking Barry for his cooperation. He noted the reassuring smile his wife gave him and hoped his instincts were correct.

"Grant Wagner," he called. Grant walked forward with a confidence he didn't feel.

\*\*\*\*\*

"You've met Samantha," said Barry, returning to his wife. "They didn't call you in for questioning, did they, Samantha?"

"No, I came here for moral support."

Megan walked over to the small group. "After what Samantha has been through, I hope they won't grill her," she said and explained Samantha's ordeal with Brad Taylor to the Klines.

"Don't judge the man too harshly," pleaded Samantha. "I don't believe he intended to hurt me. His life has not been a happy one and he deserves our pity."

\*\*\*\*\*

Rachel and Melvin Kessler were hovering in a corner of the waiting room. It was obvious they were having words, but managed to keep their voices low.

"Melvin, I don't want to see you anymore; why can't you get that through your thick skull? What we had was fun, but it's over now."

"Rachel, you were crazy about me a few days ago; is it that cop? What kind of hold has he got on you? You should be acting like the grieving widow and instead you're mooning over Samantha's husband."

"I'm not a grieving widow, Melvin. I'm not a widow at all. My marriage to Reggie was a sham. We weren't legally married and he left me with nothing."

"What do you mean you weren't legally married? You lived with the old man for years. You're entitled to some of his money."

"He gave it all to his daughter long before he died it turns out. The man left nothing to me or anyone else. I hated Reggie; if Grant hadn't killed him, I'd have done it myself. Now, get out of my face. I don't want to look at you anymore."

Melvin was shocked; he'd planned on paying off his gambling debts with Reggie Crenshaw's money. He should have bilked it out of Rachel months ago when Reggie was still alive and doling out the cash. What would he do now? Those guys he owed didn't mess around.

*****

"Mr. Wagner, where were you when you saw the body in the pool?"

Grant was nervous, but kept his voice steady when he answered Detective Bellamy's question. "Rachel Ross had instructed me to rewrite the screenplay of Samantha's book. I didn't want to do it. The first version I'd written deviated from the story quite a bit, but she wanted something *totally* different. My first instinct was to tell her to shove it, but if I'd refused, it would have been the end of any chance I had of making it out here. You see, the first time I saw Rachel, I was mesmerized by her. She was a beautiful woman, but after I got to know her, I saw her beauty was only skin deep. I changed the script as ordered and used the study where a printer had been set up. Then I went back to get my computer, and when I looked out the glass doors, I saw Mr. C floating face down in the pool. I didn't know it was Mr. C at the time. It was just a body—I didn't know who. Now, because of Mr. C, my dreams were shattering before my eyes. I'm not sure I'd have tried to help him if I'd known it was him. I know that makes me sound like a jerk, but I want to be honest with you, Detective."

"You aren't a jerk at all, Mr. Wagner. You did attempt to save the man's life even after you saw his face when you pulled him from the pool. You're free to go. Don't give up on the writing just because this didn't work out."

"Thanks, Detective. I won't give up writing, but I'm afraid I'll have to give up California; I'm flat broke."

Pete thought it ironic that most everyone working on the movie needed money. Rachel Ross didn't necessarily need money when the man she thought she'd married was alive, but now that he was dead, she was out of luck and out of cash. He decided to call her in next.

"Okay, copper, ask away; I have nothing to hide," said Rachel when she plopped down in the chair across from him with her short skirt pulled up to the top of her thigh.

Pete had been a detective for many years, but was not immune to the charm of a beautiful woman. He cleared his throat when he asked his first question.

Carol Hughes tried to suppress a smile as she watched her boss fight his reaction to the scantily clad Ms. Rachel Ross.

Pete regained his composure. "Tell me about your relationship with Reggie Crenshaw."

"Boy, you get right to the point, don't you detective? That snake, Reggie, made a fool out of me and I'll never forgive him for that. Well, I wouldn't ever forgive him if he was still alive. Now I'll just have to have the satisfaction of spitting on his grave."

"Even though you weren't legally married, you assumed you'd inherit his estate? Is that correct?"

"Of course. That's an assumption anyone would make. Who'd have guessed he'd give it all away to some kid I'd never heard of? I thought I was Reggie's first and only wife. We never talked about having kids. I didn't think he wanted them and *I* sure didn't want any. That wife of his must be a piece of work to let him live with another woman for five years and not show herself. I'll bet he was paying her to keep her mouth shut."

Pete felt the urge to correct her statement about Alexandra, but forced himself to dismiss the comment. His mind wandered to Alexandra. She and Rachel Ross couldn't have been any more different. Alexandra was warm and loving, whereas Rachel was totally self-centered.

"Ms. Ross, you left the mansion premises, but circled around and came back. Why did you do that?"

"I left because Reggie was going to sic Ivor on me. Ivor hates me and I hate him. The big lug can pick me up and carry me anywhere he wants to. I know, from experience, what kind of brute he is. In the past I've slugged him and slapped him as hard as I could and it doesn't even faze him at all. He's an animal. Anyway, I drove around the building and out of Ivor's sight because I wanted to talk to Reggie. I knew I could convince him that the story of the beauty and the cop would be a smash hit if he'd only let us continue. I wasn't looking forward to love scenes with Brad Taylor, but I was willing to sacrifice for the sake of the movie. I never got to tell him that because I walked in on Grant Wagner with his hands around Reggie's neck, strangling him."

"Why were you reluctant to act with Brad Taylor?"

"He's strange, don't you think? I've heard stories that he killed his sister so he could have their mother all to himself. If you ask me, that mother and son relationship was weird."

"Have you ever seen Brad Taylor behave in an inappropriate or threatening way?"

"Brad behaving in a threatening way? No, of course not; he's nothing like he appears on screen. He always played a macho guy, but in real-life he's a pussycat. Do you think he killed Reggie?"

Pete didn't answer the question and excused Rachel after another fifteen minutes of questioning. It was obvious that Rachel wasn't about to give up on Fletch. She brought his name into the conversation repeatedly. He had sympathy for Fletch and Samantha; this broad was determined to get her claws into Fletch again.

*****

"Mr. Kessler, how much have you had to drink this morning?"

"Is that part of your interrogation, Mr. Detective, sir?" Melvin said sarcastically. "I don't see why my drinking habits are any of your concern."

"They are my concern if you're driving an automobile in your condition."

"I don't drive drunk and I'm insulted that you'd think that I would. Don't you know drinking and driving is dangerous?"

"*I* know it's dangerous; I want to make sure you know it too. Why don't you tell me about your relationship with Reggie Crenshaw's wife?"

"Is that your business? Rachel and I are not in a relationship—at least not any more; she only has eyes for that cop out there. Why did he have to come to town? Rachel and I had a good thing going until he showed up."

Pete detected sadness in Kessler's eyes. Is it possible the guy was actually in love with Rachel? He sounded like a defeated man to Pete.

"Mr. Kessler, tell me about your back alimony and child support payments."

"Okay, I'm a little behind. Those hags took advantage of me. Why can't they go out and get jobs? I thought they'd get married again and I'd be off the hook. As far as the kids go, I never wanted them. I was tricked into fatherhood."

"What about your gambling debts? Were you tricked into betting on the wrong horses?"

"Yeah, my bookie steered me wrong. Next time I'll follow my hunches."

"Mr. Kessler, it's none of my business, but I'd suggest you give up drinking and playing the ponies, and concentrate on paying your obligation to your wives and children. The courts don't look kindly on a man who fails to support his offspring. Your gambling debts are another matter and I'm sure you know what will happen if you renege on those."

*****

After the interrogations were over and everyone left, Pete called Samantha and Fletch into his office.

"Thanks for waiting. I wanted to talk to you about Ivor. We haven't been able to find him. The maid said there are a few items missing from his bedroom in Reggie's apartment. We have an APB out for him, but I think we have all the information from him that we're going to get. I believe him when he said he was sleeping when Reggie was injured. The poor guy doesn't appear to have enough brain cells left to lie. He was a boxer and suffered from numerous concussions before he was forced to give it up and become a body guard for Reggie Crenshaw.

"Samantha, I know you're convinced of Brad Taylor's innocence, but he's the only possible suspect. I believe the others are innocent of any crime." Pete held up a photograph of the antique clock that had been in Brad's possession. "I showed each one of them this photo and asked if they recognized it. The only one who had any reaction was Rachel. She looked at it and said it was old and ugly and she'd seen enough of old and ugly being married to Reggie. She doesn't much like that guy," he said smiling.

"No, she's set her sights on my husband," said Samantha."

"You don't have a thing to worry about," said Pete. "We have Brad in a holding cell; he's been asking to see you. If you'd rather not, I understand."

"I'd like to see him. I think the poor guy could use a friend. Maybe he'll tell me something that will help clear him. It's worth a try."

## CHAPTER 17

"Samantha," Brad said when he saw her walk through the door. He wanted to touch her hair, but there was a glass wall between them. He had to pick up a telephone to talk to her.

"Hi, Brad; are you feeling all right? Are the guards being nice to you?"

"Yes, everyone is nice; they're waiting for the doctor to come and then I can go home. Will you come back to the secret room with me?"

"I can't do that, Brad; we don't belong in that room. A nice man owns the house and we can't go back."

"That's too bad. Guess what, Samantha? My sister is coming to see me. Mama was wrong; she isn't in the gutter after all. She lives in Wisconsin and she's a grandmother. What do you think about that?" He giggled like a young boy.

"I'm happy for you, Brad; I know how much you love your sister."

"Yes, I do. Mama says she's a nasty girl who does bad things, but I want to see her. Do you think Mama will be mad at me?"

"I don't think your mama will be mad at all. Sally is her child too and mothers love their children." Samantha knew that was not always the case, but what harm would a little white lie do. Mrs. Lee was not in any position to dispute her words.

"I have to go now, Samantha; they are bringing my lunch. I hope it's a peanut butter sandwich. I like peanut butter sandwiches, don't you, Samantha?"

"Peanut butter sandwiches are my favorite too, Brad," Samantha tried holding back the tears; her heart ached for the man she feared was going to kill her just a few hours ago.

*****

"I'm afraid I didn't get anything from him, Detective Bellamy; he's excited about his sister coming to visit. Is it true or a figment of his imagination?"

"It's true; the sheriff from the town she's living in called me. Sally Rafferty is her married name and she's anxious to see her brother. She and her husband are flying in later tonight. The sheriff got quite an earful from the sister. Evidently life was not pleasant in the Lee household. Sally escaped from that environment before it did any permanent damage; unfortunately, her brother was not as lucky."

"That's sad; I'd like to see Brad again, if possible. I have the feeling he knows something and it'll come out eventually. Maybe his sister will be able to get him to open up. I should have asked him about the clock, but I was afraid he wouldn't want to talk about it."

*****

Pete picked up the telephone in his office after everyone had left. Overnight he'd memorized Alexandra's number and called her.

Alexandra saw it was the police station calling and was happy to hear Pete's voice. "You're calling earlier than I thought; I hope that doesn't mean you're stuck at the station tonight."

"No, I'm done, and I'll be out the door as soon as I hang up. Are you hungry? I thought we could go to a restaurant close to your house if that's all right with you."

"I have a roast ready to put in the oven and I hoped you wouldn't mind eating at home. It's been a long time since I've cooked for a man, so you'll be taking your chances. I can whip up a couple of martinis before we eat, that way if the meal is terrible, you won't notice."

"That sound wonderful; it's been a long time since I've had a home cooked meal, and the martinis sound good too. I'm on my way."

Thirty minutes later, Alexandra heard his car pull into the driveway. She tried not to run to the door, but she was anxious to see him again.

He stood on the porch with a bouquet of wilting flowers in his hand. "Sorry about these, I bought them at a roadside stand; it's getting dark out there and I didn't see their condition."

"They're beautiful," she said and meant every word. "I'll put them in water and they'll perk up in no time."

Pete followed her into the kitchen where she had just put the roast in the oven. She filled a vase with water and reached for her cocktail shaker. "Do you like it straight up or on the rocks?" she asked.

"Better make it on the rocks; I'm driving," he said, thinking he might not be driving home tonight after all.

Alexandra smiled as though she could read his mind. "Any luck with the case? I shudder when I think what Brad Taylor could have done to Samantha in that sound-proof room."

"We aren't any closer to discovering who caused Reggie's injuries; I'm afraid Brad is the only remaining suspect although Samantha disagrees. I think she has good instincts and I'm leaning toward that conclusion myself. The trouble is, I have nothing else to go on."

"Someone must have seen or heard something; it's a big place but there were several people there."

"Samantha thinks Brad saw something that he's either ignoring or forgetting; she visited with him earlier and will try to talk to him again. I don't know how long we can hold him. She isn't pressing charges for kidnapping. I'm afraid the man needs psychiatric help, but we can't enforce it without his cooperation. How is Gina holding up?"

"Gina is better than fine; I know it sounds cold-hearted, but Reggie has been out of our lives for a long time. He was nothing more than an acquaintance to Gina. I know that sounds strange because he turned over his estate to her. It makes me wonder if he didn't have a premonition about his death."

"Maybe it wasn't so much a premonition as a fear of what Rachel was capable of. I couldn't help but compare the two of you today when I met with her. There's no comparison; you're a hard act to follow."

"I'm not sure Reggie would agree with that; I'm not sure why he married me. Back then he had any number of women who would have been the fun-loving wife he wanted. It wasn't until after Gina was born that I had to admit to myself that I was just infatuated with the man and not in love with him."

Pete smiled, hoping that statement didn't apply to him. He had to tell himself to go slow. He wanted to tell her he loved her and wanted to spend the rest of his life with her. It was hard to believe they'd only known each other for two days.

"Gina and young Mr. Lambert seemed to be hitting it off today."

"Yes, they are. When I talked to Gina today, she said they were having dinner together. He seems like a nice fellow; he's planning to tear down the bookcases in the study and opening that secret room up. Gina said he feels terrible about not examining the blueprints before this. If he'd known about the secret room he'd have torn it out, and Samantha wouldn't have been in danger. He told Gina some of the stories his grandmother had told him. That woman had an imagination; it's too bad she didn't write them down. Maybe Samantha could use them in a sequel to Professor Stonehill's memoirs."

"Maybe Blake should take her stories seriously; he would never have thought to look in that room if his grandma hadn't mentioned it. I suppose a hidden camera is too much to ask," said Pete.

"I doubt they had the technology for hidden cameras in those days."

"That's too bad. I could forget about this case and concentrate on you. I think I'll do just that," he said as he put his arms around her shoulders and drew her close, kissing her welcoming lips.

*****

"My mother was waiting for Detective Bellamy to arrive when I called her. She was almost giddy," Gina told Blake when they were driving to the restaurant.

"I like your mother, Gina; she's an older version of you. I never thought when I agreed to meet with the manager of Reggie Crenshaw's estate that it would be someone who looks like you."

"Were you expecting me to look like my father? I'm lucky I take after my mother."

"I'm lucky too; I don't think I'd want to have dinner with a female Reggie Crenshaw. I'm sorry, Gina; that's insensitive of me."

"Blake, I'm not offended. My father was a playboy and a user. He used my mother and then left her with a baby to raise on her own. Mom never took a dime from him after he left; it's not that he didn't try to buy her off; she simply refused to take his money. I think she's been a good influence on me because I don't want his money either. When he was alive, he drew what money he needed, and I didn't pay much attention to where it was going. Now that he's gone, I'd like to start a foundation and give to folks who need a helping hand. I'd also like to fund making a real film using Samantha's book. I think it's a story that begs to be told on screen. Maybe it won't make a lot of money because there aren't any mass shootings or car crashes or nudity in it the way it's written, but I don't care. What do you think?"

"I think it's a terrific idea. I read Samantha's book after I bought the house in Seabrook Shores. There are a few of us left in the world who simply like a good story and the telling of the Stonehill family qualifies."

"I only have one request—that Rachel Ross or Rochelle Rousseau as she called herself, is not a part of it."

"I don't think Samantha will disagree with you on that score," Blake said with a laugh.

\*\*\*\*\*

"Samantha, why don't we order room service tonight?" said Megan. "You've been through so much today."

"I'm fine. I thought we were going to try that Greek restaurant we saw the other day. I didn't have much lunch and when Brad talked about a peanut butter sandwich it made my mouth water."

"Greek sounds good," said Mike. "I'm game if you are, Fletch."

"It's unanimous, let's go."

\*\*\*\*\*

Brad was eating his peanut butter sandwich. It wasn't on the menu at the jail that evening but the guard who was watching him took pity on him and had her daughter make a couple of sandwiches to bring to the jail. Brad was childlike and hard for the hardened staff to ignore.

*I hope I see Samantha tomorrow*, he thought to himself. *I forgot to tell her what I saw. I should have helped mean Mr. Crenshaw, but I thought he'd get mad at me and make me leave my secret room. I didn't like all that yelling; I remember when Mama yelled at Sally. It was scary; Mama didn't yell at me like that because I always did what she told me to. Sally shouldn't sass Mama; that's why Mama told her to go away and never come back. Mr. Crenshaw yelled too. He told her to go away*

*and she wasn't getting any money from him. She was cry-
ing and then she picked up the clock and threw it at him.
He grabbed his head with his hand and there was blood.
He opened the door to the patio and she watched him go,
then she ran out the other door. I picked up the clock and
hid it so that nobody would know what she'd done. I like
her; she's pretty. I don't want her to go to jail.*

## CHAPTER 18

Pete Bellamy woke up with a start. He didn't know where he was for a minute and then remembered being in Alexandra's house. He realized he was on the sofa with a warm blanket cover him.

"Good morning, Detective," Alexandra called from the kitchen.

"What happened?" he asked.

"I suspect the second martini and the filling dinner put you to sleep. I hope it wasn't my company."

"Dinner was fantastic; did I tell you that last night?"

"Yes, you did and then promptly fell asleep. I took the liberty of removing your shoes and covered you up with my grandmother's quilt. I tried to talk you into sleeping in the guest room, but you were out like a light."

"I'm so sorry, Alexandra. I guess I didn't know how tired I was. I won't impose any longer; I'll be on my way."

"Don't be silly; I always have a couple of extra toothbrushes in the guest bathroom. Freshen up if you'd like and then come have some coffee. I'll make us some scrambled eggs."

"My car has been parked in your driveway all night. What will your neighbors say?"

"They'll say it's about time the old girl had an overnight guest, and we won't tell them it was strictly platonic. I didn't realize you were such a prude, Detective."

"I'm just mad at myself for sleeping through what could have been a very enjoyable evening."

*****

Samantha woke with the sound of the telephone. Fletch let her sleep in this morning; it was almost nine o'clock.

"Who was that calling?" she asked, trying to keep from yawning.

"It was Gina; she wants to set up a meeting with you, Barry, and Grant. She didn't say what it was about, but she sounded excited. I said you'd call her back."

"Why did you let me sleep so long? I wanted to go to the jail and meet Brad's sister. I hope I'm not too late."

Samantha showered and put her wet hair in a ponytail. She dialed Gina's number.

"Samantha, hi; I hope I didn't wake you when I called earlier."

"You didn't," Samantha lied. "What can I do for you?"

"I want to meet with you, Barry and Grant this morning, or as soon as everyone can get together. It dawned on me last night that your book should be made into a movie after all. I don't want the story to change and I don't want Rachel or Melvin involved in any way. Does that sound like something you'd be in favor of?"

"That sounds too good to be true, Gina. I believed your father was backing my book before, but it turned out Rachel wanted it her way. I know your father bought the rights to my book and now it's yours. You say you want to follow the book. I'd love it if you would, but I can't stop you if you change it."

"I'm not my father and I'm definitely not Rachel. Blake agrees that it should be kept as close to the story as possible. I want you involved; can I count on you?"

"Yes, of course. Grant and Barry both need the money and I think they'll agree also".

"I know Grant was hoping to earn enough money to keep him in Los Angeles, but why does Barry need money, if I'm not being too nosy?"

"I don't think he'd mind if I told you the medical expenses from his son's illness has almost wiped him out. He's having a difficult time financially and the movie would have been a lifesaver for him."

"That's no problem. If they agree, I'll advance them what they need. Remember, this is my father's money and I'm determined to spend it on good causes. I think both those fellows are deserving of a signing bonus."

"Gina, you're a lifesaver. Tell me when you want to meet and I'll get right on it. I'd like to talk with Brad Taylor's sister; she was supposed to arrive in town last night. I thought I could catch her at the jail. Other than that, I'm free."

"Let's make it for two o'clock. If you have their numbers, I'll call them myself. You get down to the jail. You don't want to miss Brad's sister."

"Thanks, Gina; call me if there's a change of plans."

"I got the drift of that conversation," said Fletch. "Are you sure you want to be involved in another production?"

"I don't have much choice since my manuscript belongs to Gina now. I could write the screenplay myself, but I'd like Grant to have another chance with it."

"Shall we leave for the jail now? We can stop for a breakfast sandwich on the way if that's all right with you."

"That sounds good, Fletch. I didn't think I'd be hungry again after that meal last night, but I am."

*****

Pete had a quick breakfast with Alexandra and then took off for home to shower and change. He begged her forgiveness on the way out the door and kicked himself for falling asleep. "Tonight? Dinner but no martinis?" he asked.

"That sounds terrific; call me when you can." They embraced and Pete was on his way.

He got to the office in time to accept a call from Sally Rafferty. "Mrs. Rafferty, I'm glad to talk to you. Your brother is being evaluated by a psychiatric physician, but he's not being charged with a crime."

"What about the kidnapping? He did kidnap someone, didn't he?"

"Yes, but the woman doesn't want to press charges. Samantha Degan is her name and she's taken an interest in Brad."

"I've heard how people who are held against their will often fall in love with their captors."

"That's not the case, I can assure you, Mrs. Rafferty. I feel I know Samantha and she only has Brad's best interest at heart. I'm afraid Brad is in a childlike state. That's the reason for the evaluation today. If the doctor finds any sign that Brad is unable to care for himself or is endangering himself or others, he'll be admitted to the hospital for further evaluation."

"Detective, I haven't seen or spoken with my brother in close to forty years; I'm not sure he'll want to see me."

"The guards have told me he's talked about seeing you since they told him of your visit yesterday. I believe he's anxious to see you again. I've arranged for you to meet in a small conference room at the police station. It's a comfortable room with upholstered chairs and pictures on the wall; you should feel at ease there. If you'd like someone with you when Brad comes in the room, we can arrange that too."

"Thank you, Detective Bellamy. I don't think that will be necessary. My husband, Rob, is with me. I think he's all the protection I need. Rob has rented a car and we should be at the station in less than a half hour."

"Check in at the front desk and ask for Detective Bellamy."

*****

Sally was nervous when they walked into the police station. She and Rob were greeted by Samantha Degan and her husband, Detective Fletcher.

"I don't want to intrude on your meeting with your brother. I do want to assure you that Brad didn't hurt me and I will not be pressing charges. We have gotten to know each other in the last couple of days and he's a very nice man."

"Thank you for saying that, Ms. Degan. The sheriff told me about your ordeal and I'm very sorry. Is there anything you can tell me about Brad that will help when I meet him?"

"Only that Brad is childlike; he was told you were living in a gutter."

"I'm willing to bet it was my mother who told him that. I wrote letters to him and I'm sure they were destroyed before he could read them. I called and Mama told me Sonny never wanted to see me again. When I saw he was a movie star, I didn't worry about him anymore. He seemed so strong I figured Mama had backed off and let him be himself. Now I see I was wrong. It sounds like he never did overcome our upbringing."

"You seem to have come through your childhood all right. You have a nice husband and I understand you're a grandmother."

"Yes, I was the lucky one. I was taken in as a foster child shortly after I left home. The Bakers were good to me and gave me the love I never had from Mama. I don't blame Mama. I'm sure her life was never easy and she was bringing us up the best way she knew how. I have the Bakers and the Raffertys to thank for the life I have now."

"Mrs. Rafferty, Brad is waiting for you. I'll take you to him. Mr. Rafferty, I understand you'll be joining your wife. Please follow me."

Sally felt as though her tongue was blocking the air in her throat. She didn't remember this much trepidation when she gave birth for the first time.

The door opened and an older man who was her brother stood before her. She recognized his smile and dissolved in tears.

"Hello, Sally. We got old, didn't we? You still have pretty hair; may I touch it?"

Sally stepped closer so he could touch her hair. She was glad her friend, Alice, had colored it for her last week otherwise he would see the gray roots.

"It's soft. Do you remember Mama's hair? Yours is the same color. Why did you go away, Sally?"

"I'm sorry, Sonny. I wrote to you, but you didn't answer my letters. When I called, Mama said you didn't want to talk to me. I saw every movie you were in; I saw them all two times."

"Mr. Crenshaw won't let me make his movie. I don't care; I didn't like Rachel very much. Do you know I have a friend? Her name is Samantha."

"Yes, I met Samantha; she's waiting outside to see you."

"Oh good. I have something I want to tell her. I think it's important, but I can't remember what it is." He started to cry.

"It's all right, Sonny; you don't have to remember right now. Would you like me to call you Brad?"

"I think that's my name now. I'm not sure. I better go. Doc says I need to sleep. Goodbye, Sally; come back again." He opened the door and walked out.

Rob held his wife in his arms; her brother was much worse than she'd imagined.

"Oh, Rob; what did Mama do to him? He's in terrible shape. I feel so guilty for leaving him with that woman; I should have gone back for him."

"It's not your fault, sweetheart; let's talk to the doctor who's treating him. Maybe he can help you understand Sonny's condition."

*****

"Mr. and Mrs. Rafferty, I'm your brother's doctor, Matt Henderson. We have several tests scheduled for Brad to help us decide how we can best help him. I'm afraid you're seeing the result of a nervous breakdown. This has been building up in him for quite some time and culminated upon Reggie Crenshaw's death."

"Do you think my brother killed the man?" asked a tearful Sally.

"No, but I do think he saw the person who did. He keeps saying he wants to talk to Samantha about something important and then his frustration won't let him say the words. I'm recommending he be admitted to the psychiatric department of the hospital here in Los Angeles for a complete evaluation. I think he'll do so voluntarily; it would help if you urged him to get well. He was excited to see you although it overwhelmed him. Is there any way you can stay in Los Angeles for a few more days?"

"Of course, Dr. Henderson; my wife and I will stay as long as is needed."

Sally told Samantha her brother was sleeping. The doctor thought he would be out for a couple of hours and then would be transferred to the hospital. She told Sam what the doctor said about him wanting to tell his friend something important, but couldn't remember what it was. Dr. Henderson thinks it's possible Sonny is sleep deprived and it's adding to his confusion.

Samantha gave Sally her card with her cell phone number circled. "If Brad wants to talk, call me and I'll be here or at the hospital. I'm so happy he has his sister again; you are the best medicine for him."

"Thank you, Samantha; he's lucky to have you on his side."

## CHAPTER 19

Samantha and Fletch arrived at the hotel lobby a little before two o'clock. Gina, Blake, Barry and Grant were waiting for them.

Gina outlined the plan. She told Grant she wanted the script as close to the book as humanly possible. "Barry, I have some actors in mind for the part of Professor Stonehill. I'd like to know what you think and I trust you'll be able to contact the right people to get the word out. I want Samantha to be a level-headed, serious writer and not a sex kitten. There will be no hint of impropriety between the professor and Samantha. Under no circumstance will Rachel or Melvin be involved in the production.

"I want you both to look over these contracts I had my father's lawyer draw up. If you have any questions or concerns, please say something before you sign it. We will not have any misunderstandings this time around. Gentlemen, if you do sign the contract, there will be a generous signing bonus. This is not a bribe, but an incentive. I don't want either of you to have financial worries distracting you. Are we in agreement?"

"I don't need to read it; I'm in," said Grant.

"Not so fast, Grant," repeated Gina. "I want you to read it and have it looked over by an attorney. Now, shall we forget the serious chatter and enjoy a drink by the pool?"

"One drink and then I'm going to track down a guy from my apartment building," said Grant. "He's a third-year law student and I'll have him look over the contract.

While he's doing that, I'll start the script I wanted to do in the first place."

"I know a few attorneys in the business; I'll find one and get back to you, Ms. Crenshaw," said Barry.

"Please call me Gina; I hope we'll all be friends before this adventure is over."

Grant and Barry each had a quick drink and excused themselves.

"I think you've started the ball rolling, Gina," said Samantha.

"I hope so. Did I seem too harsh with Grant? He's young and impulsive. I don't want him jumping into this thing and regretting it. I think the contracts are fair, but if they want something changed, I'm willing to consider it."

Megan and Mike joined the party. "I think Samantha should play herself; I don't think anyone could do it better than she does," said Megan.

"You'd be great in the part," laughed Fletch.

"I don't think so," said Samantha, scowling at the two of them. "I want this movie to make some money for Gina, not cost her a fortune when moviegoers ask for their money back. Let's change the subject. Blake, do you remember an ornate clock that sat on the credenza in the study?"

"I can't say I do; I lost interest in the place after having to repair a lot of plumbing and electrical problems. I intend to get rid of all the junk the last people decorated with, but haven't done it yet. The study was the only place where the furniture was normal. I spent most of my time in that room. I don't recall there being anything on the credenza except my ice bucket and fifth of whiskey."

"I think you'd remember this clock; it was something you wouldn't forget if you saw it. Megan, do you remember seeing the clock when Myra showed us around the place?"

"I'm sure I didn't. I do remember seeing it when Detective Bellamy took it from Brad. That was the first time I'd seen it."

"It was on the credenza when I went in the study in the morning. Then after Reggie's death, I had the feeling something was missing. That was the reason I returned to the study; I wanted to see if I could remember what I'd seen the day before. Brad was holding it in his hand and he asked if that was what I was looking for. I was convinced he'd hit Reggie with it, but now I don't believe he's capable of violence."

"Who's Myra?" Fletch asked.

"Myra's the stager who was going to replicate some of the rooms in Stonehill Manor," replied Samantha. "I wonder if Detective Bellamy knows her role in the movie."

Samantha's cell phone sounded. Sally Rafferty was calling. "Hello, Sally. Is Brad all right?"

"He begged me to call you, Ms. Samantha; he said he must tell you something. He won't tell me what it is and only wants to talk to you. Is there any way you can come back to the jail again; I hate to disturb you, but he's terribly agitated."

"I'll be there as soon as I can; thanks for calling, Sally."

Samantha and Fletch excused themselves. Samantha hoped that Brad would remember what he wanted to tell her this time.

When they arrived at the police station, Brad smiled. "I know what I wanted to tell you, Samantha," he said proudly. "Mr. Crenshaw came into the study; I was watching from the peephole. I could hear them because the bookcase was open just a little bit. Mr. Crenshaw didn't know about the secret room so he didn't know I was watching and listening. The lady said she'd found a clock at an estate sale and she was excited to show it to him. She picked it up and he said, 'That's the ugliest thing I've ever seen. Get it out of here and you go with it. The movie's off.'

"She said: 'You can't do that; we have a contract.'

"'Read the fine print, lady; I'm not obligated to pay you or anyone else involved in that stupid movie.'

"'But, I've spent a thousand dollars of my own money!' she yelled back at him. 'What am I supposed to do with all this beautiful furniture?'

"'I don't care what you do with it; just get out of my sight. You people are all leeches and I'm sick of the lot of you. Get out!'

"The lady was still holding the clock in her hand and she bonked Mr. Crenshaw on the noggin. I wanted to laugh because he deserved it, but I didn't want him to know I was there. He turned around and stared at her. I think it scared her and she dropped the clock before she ran out the door. Mr. Crenshaw put his hand on the back of his head and there was blood on it. He walked out the patio door and I picked up the clock and hid it in the secret room. I was afraid the lady would be in trouble if Mr. Crenshaw reported her to the police and they found the clock. She seemed like a nice lady and Mr. Crenshaw was really mean to her."

"Did I do the right thing, Samantha?"

"You did the right thing, Brad. Would you be willing to tell Detective Bellamy what you just told me?"

"I don't know; he'll be mad because I hid the clock."

"He will understand you did what you thought was best for the lady. He won't be mad."

"All right, I'll tell him. Will you be with me, Samantha?"

"Yes, I'll be with you, Brad."

\*\*\*\*\*

Samantha was relieved to know Brad hadn't harmed Reggie. She and Fletch sat with Brad while they waited for Detective Bellamy to arrive.

Brad described what he saw the day Reggie had suffered his head injury. He was relieved when the detective didn't scold him for hiding the clock from the police. Pete was gentle with the witness and avoided probing for answers.

Brad was obviously emotionally drained after he'd told his story, and an attendant escorted him back to his cell while waiting for his transfer to the hospital.

*****

"Do you have any reason to doubt his story, Samantha."

"No, Pete; I believe he was being honest. In all the excitement, I'd forgotten about Myra Simms. She was quite pushy when we met a few days ago. That was the only time I saw her at the mansion. I chose from a variety of room sketches and thought her work was done until it was time to begin filming."

"It shouldn't be too difficult to track the woman down. Thanks for your help, Samantha; I'm sure Brad was able to open up because of your friendship with him."

*****

"My crime-solving wife has done it again," said Fletch.

"I can't take credit for this one; Brad was an eyewitness and he gets the bragging rights."

"He would have taken that information to his grave if you hadn't stood by him until he felt comfortable telling the truth about what took place. I hope he can get the help he needs."

"I think he will; he has endeared himself to the staff here at the jail and that's not easy to do. His sister and brother-in-law are on his side and he has us. Maybe with friends around him, he will overcome some of the damage his mother did to him for years."

\*\*\*\*\*

It didn't take long for Pete to track down Ms. Myra Sims. He and Officer Hendricks arrived at her front door shortly after five o'clock in the evening.

"I've been expecting you, officers. I knew Reggie Crenshaw would be pressing charges against me. I have no excuse for my behavior; I was devastated when he called off the movie. My whole career dissolved that day and I'm facing financial ruin. I'm sorry I hurt him; if you need to arrest me, go right ahead." Myra held out her arms, waiting for handcuffs to be placed on them.

Pete wasn't sure what to make of this woman. Was she playing a game? Or was she truly not aware of Reggie Crenshaw's death?

"We're here to ask you some questions, Ms. Simms. We can do it here or at the station, it's your choice."

"Ask away, Detective. I'm sure Reggie told you what happened. I'm not going to lie; I'm guilty of assault and I know I must be punished. I will repent by spending time in prison because I spent my last dollar purchasing furnishings for a movie that will never see the light of day."

She led them into her living room. The drapes were drawn and there was only a sliver of light coming through the windows as the sun was beginning to set.

"Ms. Simms, have you listened to the television or read a newspaper in the last few days?"

"No, I've been wallowing in self-pity since Reggie Crenshaw dashed my dreams. I'm an artist, Detective. I tend to be overly dramatic in my reactions. You're the first human contact I've had since that awful day when I threw that beautiful antique clock in a fit of rage. I didn't intend to hit him with it; I was aiming for the window, but he got in the way."

Pete couldn't tell whether Myra Sims was oblivious or she was pretending to be. If it was the latter, she was exceptionally good at it.

"Ms. Sims, are you aware that Reggie Crenshaw is dead?"

Myra's mouth flew open and she let out an ear-splitting scream. "No, that can't be; there was blood, but he was still standing. I thought he'd kill me, so I ran. Please tell me he isn't dead."

"I want you to tell us everything that happened that afternoon. You might want to call a lawyer before you answer any questions."

"I don't have any money for a lawyer. If I killed a man, I deserve to be punished. I'll tell you everything you want to know," Myra said through her sobs.

She proceeded to tell her account of the incident. It was almost identical to the report made by Brad Taylor earlier. Pete Bellamy had no choice but to arrest her for assault. Whether she was responsible for Reggie Crenshaw's death would have to be determined by the prosecutor in the case.

# CHAPTER 20

Gina wrote two checks as signing bonuses. Barry Kline and Grant Wagner both did as she'd asked and had an attorney look over the contracts.

"I want you fellas to know, these are signing bonuses. As I told you before I want your full attention to the project and I don't want you worrying about finances". Andie Kline accompanied her husband to the meeting with Gina and Blake.

"I wanted to thank you in person, Ms. Crenshaw, for giving my husband back his peace of mind."

"Andie, I'd like for all of us to be friends. Please call me Gina. I'm not proud of the pain my father caused and I'm trying to make up for some of his behavior. The man never had a financial worry in his life, but I don't believe he was ever truly happy."

"Grant, I want you to take your time with the screenplay. I hope you're able to work all the characters into the final draft. Barry, have you thought of actors we can approach once the screenplay is written? I want a producer you can work easily with. It's unfortunate about the woman who was designing the sets; maybe we can rehire her if she's acquitted in Father's death. If not, we will use the items she purchased and reimburse her for them. That should help with her legal expenses."

Samantha was impressed with the way Gina took over this project. She knew how she wanted to proceed and was good at issuing orders without being insulting.

"Gina, my girlfriend, Jennifer, is on her way to California," said Grant. "She said if I wasn't coming home, she would come to me, I promise, I will not let her being here interfere with my writing."

"Grant, I don't expect anyone to give up their life for this project. I want all of you to live your lives. If it takes years to accomplish a finished product, so be it. When are we going to meet your girl?"

"Very soon, I'll pick her up at the airport in two hours," Grant said unable to suppress his smile.

*****

Gina hired a lawyer to represent Myra Sims. Because Reggie had died after a fall in the pool, the prosecution couldn't prove Myra was responsible for his death. She was charged with accidental bodily injury to a human being and required to attend an anger management course and serve two hundred hours of community service. The judge was influenced by her obvious remorse.

*****

With the movie project in the capable hands of Gina, Barry, Grant, Samantha, Fletch and their friends finally enjoyed their California vacation. They were busy for a full week before it was time to go back to Lancashire and resume their lives.

They arrived during a snowstorm in early March and remembered fondly lounging at the pool the day before. They had made good friends and would never forget their time in California.

EPILOGUE

With the love and support of his sister Sally, Brad was released from the psychiatric unit of the hospital in Los Angeles. He moved to the small town in Wisconsin to be with Sally and Rob's family. He helped in the diner and participated in community activities including plays put on by the locals. Everyone was happy to have a real movie star as a part of their town, and Brad became a very social and popular addition to the community. He and Sally's friend, Alice, were often together. He and Samantha talked on the phone once or twice a month. Samantha was his only friend at one time and he would always have a special place in his heart for her.

Rachel reluctantly gave up on the idea of having Fletch in her life. He'd made it abundantly clear that he had no interest in her. It didn't take long before Rachel found a replacement for Reggie Crenshaw. She hired a lawyer to verify that her marriage to the seventy-five-year-old was legal and that she was his only heir.

Pete Bellamy and Alexandra Crenshaw admitted their attraction for each other was the real thing and were married in a small chapel in the town of Seabrook Shores where they'd met only a few months earlier.

Blake Lambert didn't sell his grandmother's mansion after all. He and Gina turned it into a five-star restaurant. The secret room was perfect for a wine cellar and now had a door that was visible from the room that once was a study. The pool was filled in and became an area for outside dining. The outside of the mansion was photographed and used in the movie. The inside sets were designed in the studio with Myra Sims in charge of their authenticity. Blake closed his London office and moved permanently to California to be with his wife, Gina, and to await the birth of their first child.

Megan and Mike were married in a quiet ceremony in her hometown with Samantha and Fletch as their matron of honor and best man. Megan's mother tried her best to keep the reception small, but with so many friends and family in the small town, it was impossible. Megan didn't care how large the reception was because she was marrying Mike and that was all that mattered.

Barry and Andie Kline's son's cancer remained in remission. He wasn't out of the wood completely, but each day that passed got him closer to a full recovery. Barry was happy directing a film that was worthwhile. He was thankful to Samantha and Gina for giving him a chance.

Grant finished the screenplay and he and Jennifer returned to Iowa where they were married. Grant worked as a mechanic in his father's garage and wrote suspense novels during his time off. With the money he'd made writing the screenplay, he was able to have his book published. It was mildly successful and he felt he had the best of both worlds. He and Jennifer were looking forward to a vacation in California when they would attend the premier of *Stonehill Manor*.

Melvin Kessler's debts continued; he was out of work and out of money. He felt he had no choice but to run from the law and his bookie. He disappeared and has not been heard from since.

The movie premier was scheduled three days before Valentine's Day. Megan and Mike were unable to attend because Megan was in her ninth month of pregnancy. Samantha was happy for her friend but would miss her being there.

Samantha looked like a movie star in her full-length silver lamé dress and matching shoes. She walked the red carpet, hoping she wouldn't trip in her spiked high heels. Fletch felt uncomfortable in a tuxedo, but was extremely proud of his wife.

The critics raved about the movie; some called it refreshing, some called it a classic, some said there wasn't a dry eye in the house. Samantha was happy with the reaction, but knew this would be her first and last venture into Hollywood. She was a small-town girl and liked it best that way.

Gina threw a party and invited everyone who had anything to do with the movie from the actors to the people who delivered food to the set. She was doing her best to spend every bit of her father's money, but found she'd made more money than when she'd started. She would continue to find worthy causes and help strangers without their knowledge.

When Samantha and Fletch were in California, Megan gave birth to a baby girl. She was sorry her best friend couldn't be with her, but they both knew babies had their own timetable.

Samantha and Fletch returned home once again. Samantha vowed to never be involved in another real-life mystery. "I'll only write about murders from now on."

Fletch had his doubts; mysteries seemed to fall into her world and that was something he loved about her despite himself.

THE END

## ABOUT THE AUTHOR

 Jane O'Brien is a wife, mother of three, and grandmother of five. Jane and her husband, Dave, have lived in several states in their over fifty years of marriage. They are retired and live in Northern Colorado. Jane enjoys writing mysteries and family and friendship novels. *Murder in Seabrook Shores* is the fifth in the Samantha Degan Mystery series.

# Books by Jane O'Brien

*Bristol Falls*
*Glenwood Hills*
*Cumberland Heights*

*Murder in Forest Glen*
*The Mystery at Shelby Lake*
*The Mystery on Waverly Island*
*Murder in Pinewood Bluff*

*Samantha Degan Series*
*Murder in Stonehill Manor*
*Murder in Lancashire*
*Murder in Ashville*
*Murder at Seabrook Shores*

*Camden Corners Series*
*Camden Corners Part One*
*Camden Corners Part Two*
*Camden Corners Part Three*
*Camden Corners Part Four*
*Camden Corners Part Five*
*Camden Corners Part Six*